JANE EYRE

A Drama in Three Acts

Dramatised from Charlotte Brontë's Novel

by

HELEN JEROME

Samuel French—London
New York—Sydney—Toronto—Hollywood

JANE EYRE was produced at the Queen's Theatre, Shaftesbury Avenue, London, W.1, on October 13th, 1936.

CHARACTERS

JANE EYRE	Curigwen Lewis
MR. ROCHESTER	Reginald Tate
MRS. FAIRFAX	Susan Richmond
THE MANIAC	Dorothy Hamilton
GRACE POOLE (her Keeper)	F. Marriott-Watson
ADELE VARENS (a Child)	Betty Percheron
LORD INGRAM	Stanley Bell, junior
LADY INGRAM	Marjorie Chard
BLANCHE INGRAM	Yvette Pienne
BRIGGS (a Solicitor)	Cyril Vernon
REVEREND WOOD	Arthur Ridley
RICHARD MASON	Ronald Kerr
DIANA RIVERS	Mollie Shannon
ST. JOHN RIVERS	Whitmore Humphreys
LEAH	Phyllis Shand
JOHN	Frank Tickle
HANNAH	Marie Ault

THE PLAY PRODUCED BY ATHOLE STEWART

SYNOPSIS OF SCENES

ACT I

SCENE 1.—The Library at Thornfield Hall, at Milcote. An afternoon in Winter.

SCENE 2.—The same. A morning in March.

SCENE 3.—The same. Evening, a week later.

ACT II

SCENE 1.—The same. An evening in April, ten days later.

SCENE 2.—The same. A morning in May.

ACT III

SCENE 1.—Living-room at Moore House, near Whitecross. Dusk, one year later.

SCENE 2.—The same as Act I. A few days later.

STORY OF THE PLAY

OVER one hundred years ago Charlotte Brontë suddenly sent this silvery little figurine, Jane Eyre, out into the astonished world between the pages of an extraordinary novel, with its lyrically lovely singing prose and its strange, violent romantic theme.

As for the story—here is Thornfield Hall, with its bitter skies above and the wild clouds racing over them—and here is the gallant little figure of the eighteen-year-old girl with the indomitable soul " so frail yet so inflexible " who has planned her way out of the dreadful orphanage, at Lowood, and found herself " a new situation " as she gravely terms it, when Rochester asks her " Have you descended from a moonbeam."

Literature has not duplicated such a love story as follows between the embittered tragically lonely Rochester, landed proprietor and Jane's employer (as governess for his young ward, Adele Varens, who is his illegitimate daughter) and Jane, untouched and innocent but intellectually his equal.

Rochester's tragedy is the existence of an insane wife whom he has as compassionately as possible kept in the west wing of his mansion in the care of an attendant, Grace Poole, who is the only person in his household aware of the maniac's identity. He does not commit her to an asylum because, at that period, the insane were shockingly ill-treated by inhuman attendants in institutions.

Jane remains in ignorance of his terrible secret, even as the love between them grows. Feeling that he cannot give up his dream of a new life with this girl whom he has now learned to love with all the thwarted tenderness of his violent and passionate nature, Rochester decides to go through the marriage ceremony with the unsuspecting Jane.

Grace Poole secretly sends for the maniac's brother, hoping for a reward and Richard Mason, the brother, brings with him an attorney, Briggs, to whom he gives a copy of his sister's marriage certificate. The marriage ceremony is summarily stopped and the proof of Rochester's wife's existence given to the horrified clergyman.

Jane, without reproaching Rochester, and understanding and forgiving him, nevertheless refuses to remain with him and with agony in her heart because of " the laws and principles " that are part of her character, leaves him—running out of his clinging arms and out of his house.

She wanders over the moors for three nights and finally reaches the home of her cousins, the Rev. St. John Rivers and his sister, who unconscious of her kinship to them, take her in and give her a home for a year.

Meantime, Rochester, after madly searching for her, gives her up as lost and settles down to the life of a brooding savage recluse, made more so because of the loss of his eyesight a few months later, due to his heroic attempt to save his mad wife from death when, escaping from her keeper, she sets the west wing on fire. His wife was killed.

One evening at dusk, Jane, in another county, is just about to yield to a proposal from her cousin, St. John, to go with him to India, where he intends to become a missionary, only as he is careful to tell her, because she will be a great help to him in his work. She is hesitating, although now only anxious to fill her life with some useful work—when in the wild, sad cry of the wind across the moors she seems to hear her lover's voice. So certain is she that Rochester is in trouble and calling her, that she catches up her shawl and flees—returning to Thornfield.

There, she is grief-stricken to find him blind, but is welcomed with such wild joy, both by Mrs. Fairfax, his faithful housekeeper, and with, at first, incredulous rapture by Rochester—that she refuses to leave him again, and when he hesitates to ask her to marry him on account of his blindness, she perches herself on his knee and declines to budge. He then understands her true quality and when he finally asks her to kiss him she thanks him with charming humility, and does so, as she quaintly tells him, " with all her heart."

DESCRIPTION OF CHARACTERS

JANE EYRE (who Rochester says) looks like "an elf in a fairy tale," quaint, grave and arrestingly "different."

She is disconcertingly honest, incapable of flattery and with an enormous capacity for feeling. She is too intelligent not to be witty, but is so at the most unexpected moments.

She is probably the most highly individualized feminine character ever put upon the stage, and can as easily fit into her own time . . . 1847 as into the present day, because she is of the stuff of which Immortality is made.

Her age is between eighteen and nineteen, but her wisdom is so striking that one is inclined to think her a product of Reincarnation . . . an old Soul.

ROCHESTER is the first genuine caveman of literature, the epitome of manly virility, yet because of the inescapable tragedy of his life, hidden from everybody except his mad wife's attendant, he has become bitter, morose, ironical and difficult to approach. The excitement and passion between him and Jane is understandable from the very contrast between them added to the constantly alighting spark from their unusually brilliant minds.

The sudden unexpected flashes of tenderness in him build him into a figure that approaches the hidden ideal in most women, whether from 1840 or 1942.

As Jane enters his great dark house, where her destiny is waiting, demure in her dove-grey gown, her little pelisse and bonnet, and sits sedately with her little hands folded, she, whose young heart could be winged with rapture by a scrap of bird-song or a waft of honeysuckle from a moon-drenched garden, Rochester, that connoisseur of human beings, instantly recognizes in her a "clipped young eagle."

Rochester is under forty, and in his romantic clothes, his riding breeches at first entry, high stock, and black cloak, which he unclasps from his neck and throws on to a chair, it is small wonder that Jane Eyre does not recognize in him such a prosaic entity as her future employer.

MRS. FAIRFAX, housekeeper and distant relative of Rochester, whom she always thinks of as "The Master of Thornfield," to whom she is grateful for her pleasant situation, and anxious to please and make comfortable. She is merely aware that there is some relative of Mr. Rochester's who is insane and kindly protected by him in the west wing and looked after by Grace Poole.

She is a simple, well bred, gentle old lady, who senses Jane's exquisite quality as a human being.

She is an aristocratic old-world figure from whose hands one instinctively expects (and receives) courtesy, kindness and who possesses the long-lost art of making a house into a sheltered, hallowed spot.

Although elderly she is alert and tireless and nothing is done in this aristocratic household without her authority, supervision and interest.

She is usually dressed in black silk, very stiff and elegant, white lace cap and black lace mittens. Eighteenth-century voluminous skirt and fitted bodice.

In the wedding scene she wears pale grey and bonnet.

ADELE VARENS, Rochester's ward, is an extremely charming, spoiled, doll-like French child, who can be from five to seven. She is interested in Rochester for his gifts and because he represents unexpected delights to her. The theatre and the dance are in her blood as they are her heritage, and she is completely bored with anything in the nature of books or study.

She looks like a lovely doll in her billowing skirts with lace-edged drawers visible from beneath them.

In the ballet scene she wears the pale pink, petalled ballet dress and the wreath of pink roses, pink satin pumps and pink socks that Rochester has ordered to be sent her from Paris.

LEAH, the parlourmaid at Thornfield. A pert, but sweet Yorkshire lass with her eyes and ears always on the alert, and sometimes (to Mrs. Fairfax) embarrassingly aware of the mysterious goings-on in the west wing, though quite unconscious of their true significance.

Her age is twenty or so, and her dress a voluminous black, tight bodice, white muslin apron and pretty white cap. She speaks with a Yorkshire accent and never uses the article " the " in her speech.

THE MANIAC is only glimpsed once in The Mad Scene when she creeps in stealthily in the half light, in her white nightgown, her long black hair streaming and her pale disfigured face lit up by maniacal dark eyes. Her hands are long-fingered and clawlike. She is in her early thirties.

GRACE POOLE, a grim middle-aged woman of terrific force with tightly screwed back hair, and gives the suggestion that she has a secret hankering after alcohol.

(It was because of this that she later neglects her charge long enough to enable the poor mad creature to escape and set the house afire.)

There is something medieval about Grace Poole. Her voice is harsh and masculine, she exudes cruelty and has a manner that varies between cringing and truculence. She wears a dark woollen stuff dress, an apron and a sort of helmet cap that seems to turn her into a gaoler.

MASON, the Maniac's brother, is in his twenties, a pale, psychopathic-looking individual, frightened of his own shadow, but passionately determined to defend his sister's rights.

He wears a grey suit, high stock and high grey hat.

BLANCHE INGRAM, a spoiled, snobbish young woman of the period, determined to marry Rochester; haughty and overbearing and innately cruel. She fails to penetrate the studied insolence of Rochester's ironical compliments. She is in her twenties and is always exquisitely dressed in the silks and satins of the times. Her evening gown is cut off her shoulders although decorously high above the breast. It is of pale blue with silver lace outlining the shoulders and top of tight bodice. The skirt is full and long, and is covered from the knees down with little rows of silver lace and pink velvet bows. She carries a fan with charming grace. Her hair falls in curls to her neck.

LADY INGRAM, a worldly middle-aged dowager of the old school. She is only interested in achieving a suitable marriage for Blanche and has a private and not too successfully concealed contempt for her rather inept husband, whose title and estate are his chief claims to her attention.

Her evening gown is dark purple, she wears jewels, and presents an overwhelming appearance of wealth and Position.

One would think twice before beginning an argument with her. Lord Ingram usually thinks three times.

LORD INGRAM, a very etiolated, slender old gentleman, subdued in manner, as one would expect after having met his wife. He is very exquisitely turned out in his black dinner clothes, black velvet collar and snowy white lace trimmed shirt and high white stock. His military moustache is snow white.

He is always bored and invariably wants to go home where he is still more bored, but he recognizes the necessity of marrying off his rather terrifying young daughter and puts up with the visits to Thornfield, although he finds " the beds less satisfying than the dinners."

BRIGGS, a somewhat sanctimonious attorney from London, hired by Mason, and determined to prevent the bigamous marriage. It shocks his conventional mind and because of his sincerity he compels respect. He wears the usual black broadcloth of his profession, and carries an impeccable high black hat.

THE REV. WOOD, a rather lovable, shocked, bewildered little clergyman who finds the goings-on completely incredible. Everything he says he seems to be saying to himself. He is *definitely not* to be played as the stage clergyman, shocked and pompous, intoning his lines and uttering pious platitudes.

DESCRIPTION OF CHARACTERS

If he is played as indicated, it will soften the melodrama of the scene and make it more credible, also it will offer a distinct contrast to the attorney.

DIANA RIVERS, a completely charming, human and unexpectedly witty figure in the somewhat humourless household at Moor House.

Diana is in her twenties and has a slightly ironical attitude towards her serious, fanatic, Appollonian brother which is completely unsuspected by him, who is the lord of creation in the household of women . . . of that period in England.

ST. JOHN RIVERS, a very handsome, severe, but sincerely *good*, young clergyman, whose flaming mission is to become a missionary to India. He possesses no humour whatever and so regards his outrageous proposal to Jane to marry him in order to help his work as a perfectly natural one.

He is in his early twenties, and wears the clerical black of the period.

HANNAH, an elderly Yorkshire faithful and loving character, who has spent her life serving the Rivers family, the parents of her present employers. She is devoted and tyrannical, managing her two young charges, feeding and cooking for them and never dreaming of any other existence. She has all the Yorkshire suspicion and so regards even a Jane Eyre as a dangerous character on first acquaintance.

She pretends to despise the male sex, knowing something of its frailties, but deep down in her is the old idea of its superiority or at least its claim to be spared badly cooked food and any other discomforts incidental to a domestic life. " You know how gentlemen dislike their food spoilt," she tells Diana reproachfully.

She wears grey in the first scene, with cap tied with black ribbon, and apron. In the second she wears a printed cotton dress and apron and cap.

JANE EYRE

ACT I

SCENE 1

Thornfield Hall at Milcote.
The library at Thornfield. Afternoon. Winter. Dim, firelit, purple-curtained
room. At R. in the back wall is a locked door leading to the west wing; a fire-
place a little R.C. at back with bookshelves on either side; double doors L.C. at
back; windows in upper L. wall; double doors down L.
There is a console table against the R. wall; tables before the bookshelves at back;
a spinet with chair in front of the windows L.; a console table below the
windows with chairs in front and below it; a hassock or stool in front of the
fireplace; a sofa at R.C.; a table with two chairs at C.
AT RISE: MRS. FAIRFAX *seated in chair* R. *of table* C. LEAH *enters* L.C.,
curtsies. Crosses to spinet—puts vase and flowers down and goes to window.

MRS. FAIRFAX. Why, Leah, I didn't ring.

LEAH. I know, ma'am, but I'm that excited I can hardly wait for
the new governess to arrive.

MRS. FAIRFAX. You had better defer your excitement, until we find
out if it is the right one at last.

LEAH. (*Turns—Crosses a step to table* C.) Oh, but this one is English.
That means she'll be respectable at any rate.

MRS. FAIRFAX. Yes, one certainly can expect that.

LEAH. I never did 'old with them French people, ma'am. Of
course Miss Adele bein' French an' all—Naturally 'ad to have someone
who could talk all that unfortunate language. (*Over* MRS. FAIRFAX'S
shoulder.) All the same I knew that first governess was no good from
start, a right down French hussy, that's what *she* was!

MRS. FAIRFAX. Hush, Leah, not everyone can expect to be born in
England.

LEAH. (*Picks up books on table* C. *Crosses to console* R. *and puts books
down.*) More's the pity. And that second one! Ooh my gracious
she *was* a one!

MRS. FAIRFAX. I have never discovered why she left so hurriedly.
She only gave me two days' notice. I expect it is too quiet here for
French people—they are *so* upsetting.

LEAH. (*Darkly. Crosses to fireplace; picks up brush.*) That wasn't the
reason. (*Turns and looks at* MRS. FAIRFAX.)

MRS. FAIRFAX. (*Uneasily.*) Now, Leah, I hope you are not going to
start that nonsense again.

LEAH. (*Brushing up hearth.*) Nonsense, is it? I'm only saying,

1

ma'am, as there's things happening here, noises and such like, going on in this house, as no one likes to live with. The master never stays long. He don't have to stand it. (*Brush down.*) If it weren't for you, ma'am, bein' so kind an' all, I'd 'a' been off long ago myself. (*Crossing to above table.*) You know as well as I do what drove them other two away; governesses 'ave ears, same as rest of us. But bein' as she's English, belike she'll 'ave a bit o' spunk to 'er.

(*From off* R. *Door to west wing—*MANIAC—*short laugh.*)

MRS. FAIRFAX. (*With dignity.*) They were not "driven" away—unless you mean by John—in the carriage.

(MANIAC *slightly louder laugh. Door slam* R.)

GRACE POOLE. (*Off stage.*) Quiet, quiet.

(MRS. FAIRFAX *rises and goes to door* R., *tries to see if locked.*)

LEAH. (*Turns.*) What be ye doin' that for, ma'am?

MRS. FAIRFAX. Grace Poole makes far too much noise. I sometimes hear doors banging after everyone is asleep. (*Crosses to chair and sits.*) I'm glad I put Miss Eyre in the room next to Miss Adele's. It's on this side of the house.

LEAH. (*Meaningly.*) Belike, she'll sleep more soundly, ma'am.

MRS. FAIRFAX. (*Reprovingly.*) That will be all, Leah.

(*Doorbell rings off* L.)

LEAH. Ah, this will be Miss Eyre, now.

MRS. FAIRFAX. Go and see, my girl.

(LEAH *exits* L.C. MRS. FAIRFAX *rises.*)

JANE. (*Off up* L.) I'm Miss Eyre—the new governess.

LEAH. (*Excitedly. Off.*) Help the coachman with the trunk, John This way, Miss Eyre. Mrs. Fairfax is expecting you.

(LEAH *and* JANE *enter.* JANE *crosses down to* R. *of spinet and is met there by* MRS. FAIRFAX.)

MRS. FAIRFAX. How do you do, my dear?

JANE. Mrs. Fairfax?

MRS. FAIRFAX. (*Leading* JANE *below console* L.) Yes. I'm afraid you've had a tedious ride, John drives so slowly. Come near the fire, you must be cold.

JANE. (*Grateful and shy.*) Thank you, ma'am.

MRS. FAIRFAX. You can't imagine what a relief it is that you've arrived safely in this terrible weather. (*Untying* JANE's *bonnet.*) Let me take your bonnet. I dare say your fingers are numb from the cold. (*Hands bonnet to* LEAH.)

(LEAH *puts bonnet on spinet and exits down* L.)

JANE. (*With a laugh.*) I don't mind the cold. I was used to it at Lowood.

MRS. FAIRFAX. Some nice hot tea and scones will warm you. (*Seats* JANE R. *of* C. *table and crosses to sofa. Sits.*) Sit here, I think you'll be more comfortable, my dear.

JANE. (*With a sigh.*) Thank you.

MRS. FAIRFAX. You'll find life here very different from a big institution like Lowood.   How did you happen to take a situation in an orphan asylum ?   (*With curiosity.*)

JANE.   (*Simply.*)   I had no choice.   I was one of the orphans.   That is, until three years ago;—then, I began to teach.

MRS. FAIRFAX.   (*Sympathetically.*)   I don't suppose you were very happy there ?

JANE.   No, ma'am.   (*Pause.   There is one of those funny silences.   They eye each other with shy interest.*)   Shall I see Miss Fairfax soon ?

MRS. FAIRFAX.   (*Surprised.*)   Who ?

JANE.   My pupil.

MRS. FAIRFAX.   (*Laughs.*)   Oh, you mean Adele.   Adele Varens is her name.

JANE.   (*Puzzled.*)   Then she's not your own daughter ?

MRS. FAIRFAX.   (*With quaint inconsequence.*)   No, I've no family.

JANE.   Oh !   (*Dying to know who ADELE really is.*)

MRS. FAIRFAX.   But we shall try to make you happy here.   (*Rises as does* JANE.   JANE *is very puzzled.*)   Thornfield is lovely in spring and summer.   (*Crosses to hassock at fireplace and sits.*)   If only Mr. Rochester would take it into his head to reside here permanently.   Great houses require the presence of their owners.   They seem to go into mourning without them.

JANE.   (*Still more puzzled.*)   Mr. Rochester ?

MRS. FAIRFAX.   The owner of Thornfield.

JANE.   I thought it belonged to you.

MRS. FAIRFAX.   Bless you, child, I'm only the housekeeper.   I'm distantly related to Mr. Rochester; but I never presume on it.   Adele is Mr. Rochester's ward.   (*In a slightly shocked undertone that makes* JANE *smile.*)   She's French.   (*Pause.*)   He practically never comes here; he hates the place.

JANE.   (*Looking around the whole room.*)   Hates—this ?—

MRS. FAIRFAX.   He's a strange man, my dear—travels around the world most of the time.   And when he speaks to you, it's hard to know whether—he's in jest or earnest.

JANE.   (*Smiling with pleasure.*)   Oh, ironical ?

MRS. FAIRFAX.   I don't know what that word means, my dear; but if it means peculiar—he *is* not exactly *that!*   (JANE *indicates a willingness to have this explained.*   MRS FAIRFAX *hurries on.*)   But he's a gentleman, a landowner—and you know what they're like.   The last letter I received was from Sicily—a place called Taormina.   He said it was peaceful there.

JANE.   Peaceful ?   But I should think that this house was the most peaceful place on earth.   (*Sighs.   Looks around.*)   After Lowood it seems too good to be true.

MRS. FAIRFAX.   (*Intently examining* JANE.   *Pauses.   Surveys* JANE *with pleasure.*)   You are just as I expected you to be.

JANE.   (*Laughs.*)   Was my advertisement such a confession ?

MRS. FAIRFAX.   It appeared to be written by a serious girl who really wanted a situation.

Jane. Do I look as dull as that?

Mrs. Fairfax. (Puzzled.) But my dear, your references were all that could be desired. (Pause.) It will be quite pleasant now with an English companion. (Mrs. Fairfax rises. r. door lock rattles once. After a short pause—repeats. Speaking through business—slightly louder. Trying to drown the sound.)—Thornfield is a fine old hall—

Jane. (Thinking Mrs. Fairfax doesn't hear. Politely.) Isn't there someone at that door?

Mrs. Fairfax. (Quickly. Rushes words into each other nervously.) Oh, no, that leads to the unused west wing. It has been closed up for some time. Except for one room, Grace Poole uses for her sewing. Perhaps you're not accustomed to living in great houses. One is likely to be nervous—

Jane. No. I've dreamed of such a place as this.

Mrs. Fairfax. It was brave of you to plunge into an entirely new environment.

Jane. There's nothing brave in trying to escape from dullness, Mrs. Fairfax.

Mrs. Fairfax. Perhaps I'm old-fashioned. I've never felt the need of anything more exciting than my knitting or listening to some good sacred music.

Jane. The world is so wide—so many sensations are awaiting those who have the courage—Perhaps some of us are born to go and find them.

Mrs. Fairfax. And others like me to sit still—

Jane. (Smiling.) And—give out the music?

Mrs. Fairfax. (Crosses to c. table, picks up lace and turns to Jane.) Well, I'm thankful I never had the call, my dear. But I do hope you do not need excitement. We're so very quiet here. (Anxiously surveying Jane's eager face.)

Jane. I can be peaceful too. I have plenty of excitement in my own mind.

Mrs. Fairfax. Well, I'll run upstairs and see to your room. If I don't, damp sheets will be on your bed and no warmer put into it.

Jane. No one has ever been like this to me—

Mrs. Fairfax. (Crossing down to door l.) Take off your wrap and rest here until tea arrives. You won't be nervous, dear? (Gives an involuntary glance at r. door.)

(Jane shakes her head, smiles, holds l. door open for Mrs. Fairfax, who exits. Crosses to chair r. of l. table and puts coat down. Crosses to hassock, sits—looks around. Holds foot out to fire. Stares into fire.)

Rochester. (Enters l.c.; crosses to spinet, puts riding crop down and sees Jane. Stands surveying her, slightly amused, after the first surprise.) And who might you be? Where did you come from? (Crosses to up of table c.) Have you descended on a moonbeam? Or are you a discontented hamadryad escaped from your oakey prison?

Jane. (Turns on hassock.) I'm Jane Eyre. (Pause. In an explanatory addition.)—the new governess.

ROCHESTER. (*Surveys her.*) Deuce take me! The new governess! Well, aren't you dying to know who *I* am?

JANE. (*Calmly.*) No, not at all, except to wonder at your form of address, and what *you* are doing here?

ROCHESTER. (*Crosses to spinet, taking coat off; throws it on stool.*) Well—that's a famous sting for me! What indeed *am* I doing here, near the casket of my treasure? (*Turns, crosses back a step. Ironically.*) With its ivy-covered battlements, its smoothly shaven lawns, isn't it an earthly paradise?

JANE. (*Judicially.*) I've seen little of it as yet, but, it certainly seems so externally.

ROCHESTER. (*Amused. Crossing to table* C.) " Certainly seems so externally!" You are very precise in your form of expression.

JANE. It's my opinion that houses cannot be judged by externals, any more than human beings. (*Looking dead front.*) There are secret chambers in all of us.

ROCHESTER. (*With quick suspicion of possible implications—of which she is totally innocent.*) Secret chambers?

JANE. The heart has many compartments—some for others, one for oneself.

ROCHESTER. (*Stares at her incredulously.*) God bless my soul! And all these years I have wandered round the world in search of distraction!

JANE. (*Nods—decidedly.*) You must be unhappy.

ROCHESTER. Unhappy?

JANE. People who wander round the world all the time are usually running away from something.

ROCHESTER. (*After a pause, spent in contemplating her with a quizzical puzzlement.*) How old are you?

JANE. (*Turns away.*) I should have to learn your right to know as well as the reason for your curiosity.

ROCHESTER. (*Crosses down to face* JANE. *With sudden abruptness. Rudely.*) The right of your employer—and the owner of the house in which you seem to be so much at home.

JANE. (*Rises, hurriedly; curtsies.*) You must excuse me, sir. I didn't even know you were in England.

ROCHESTER. (*Brusquely; with one of his sudden changes of mood.*) Well, you know now.

JANE. (*Crosses front to get coat from* L. *chair.*) Yes, sir.

(ROCHESTER *to mantel shelf; picks up snuff box.*)

ADELE. (*Enters* L. *on finish of* JANE'S *cross. Runs to* JANE *and curtsies.*) Voici, my new governess at last! Chere Mamzelle: I 'ave been waiting longtemps to see you. 'Ow gentille you are. Les autres comme ils sont disagreeables. Oui, toutes les deux! (*Sees* ROCHESTER.) Oh, Monsieur, excuse me. I did not know you were chez nous. (*Crosses above table to* ROCHESTER; *throws her arms around him.*) Have you a present for me? (*Pauses, tries to kiss him.*) I wish to be embraced.

ROCHESTER. (*Crossing to middle of sofa.*) Which do you want most? The embrace or a peep in my travelling bag.

ADELE. (*Coaxingly.*) Cher Monsieur, you always 'ave sooch ver interesting things in it.

ROCHESTER. Adele, you're young yet to exhibit the faults of your sex.

ADELE. (*Pouts.*) Oh, but Monsieur—

MRS. FAIRFAX. (*Enters* L; *crosses below console* L. *Excitedly.*) Oh, Mr. Rochester, why didn't you let me know you were coming? I should have sent John with the carriage—to meet you on the road. Is your horse taken care of, sir?—Can I get you anything?

ROCHESTER. (*Goes to lower end of sofa; sits.* ADELE *kneels up stage of him.*) Madam, I should like some tea.

MRS. FAIRFAX. It's coming at once—Miss Eyre was just going to have some—*this* is Miss Eyre, the new governess for Adele.

ROCHESTER. (*Ignoring* JANE.) Are you being a good girl, Adele?

ADELE. (*Crossing* L; *kissing* JANE's *hand. Charmingly.*) I shall be now, I have sooch a gentille new gouvernante—

MRS. FAIRFAX. (*Anxiously.*) But Miss Eyre, sir—

ROCHESTER. (*Indifferently.*) Let Miss Eyre be seated.

(JANE *sits down* L. *and* LEAH *enters* L. *with tea things.* MRS. FAIRFAX *arranges chair* L. *of* C. *table and sits to pour tea.* ADELE *crosses up to hassock, sits. They form a typical Victorian picture, the lordly male, the three respectful females.*)

MRS. FAIRFAX. We are so glad you are home again, sir. The house is lonely without a gentleman. And now with Miss Eyre here—We shall be quite gay—

(JANE *smiles.*)

ROCHESTER. (*Very bored.*) Madam, I should like some tea.

MRS. FAIRFAX. Yes, sír. (ADELE *rises, crosses to table* C.) Miss Eyre, will you hand Mr. Rochester his tea; Adele might spill it.

(JANE *rises and is just crossing to* ROCHESTER, *as——*)

ADELE. N'est-ce pas, Monsieur, qu'il y a un cadeau pour Mamzelle Eyre dans votre petit coffre?

ROCHESTER. Cadeaux? Who talks of cadeaux? Did you expect a present, Miss Eyre? Are you fond of presents?

JANE. They are generally thought of as pleasant things.

ROCHESTER. Generally thought? But what do *you* think? (*Takes tea.*)

JANE. (*Judicially.*) I should have to *think* before answering that; a present has many facets; the giver, the motive—

ROCHESTER. Miss Eyre, you are not so unsophisticated as Adele. She demands a cadeau clamorously the moment she sees me—You—beat about the bush.

JANE. Because I have less confidence in my deserts than Adele. She can claim old acquaintance and custom, I am a stranger and have done nothing to entitle me to—

ROCHESTER. Oh, don't fall back on over-modesty. I can see you will be a good teacher for this French monkey. She is not over-bright and will need one.

JANE. (*Rises.*) Sir, you have now given me my " cadeau." (*Trace of curtsey.*) I thank you. (*Crosses* L. *to below chair* R. *of table and is stopped by* ROCHESTER.)

ROCHESTER. Where are your parents ?

JANE. I have none.

ROCHESTER. Never had any, I suppose. You were brought hither by the men in green, I daresay.

JANE. The men in green forsook England a hundred years ago. I don't think summer or harvest or winter moon will ever shine on *their* revels again.

(MRS. FAIRFAX *listens to them, perplexed at such talk.*)

ROCHESTER. (*Studying* JANE.) No wonder you have rather the look of another world—I marvelled where you got that sort of face—You make me think of fairy tales.

JANE. Fairy tales are diverting things, sir, but I have had no part in any. (*Crosses, sits in chair* L.)

(ADELE *goes to* JANE *with tea.*)

MRS. FAIRFAX. (*Fearing he is not pleased with* JANE.) I'm thankful that Providence sent Miss Eyre to us.

ROCHESTER. Oh, don't trouble yourself to give her a character; eulogizing will not bias me. She began by questioning my right of entry into my own house. (*Chuckles.*) You have never lived in a town, have you, Miss Eyre ?

JANE. (*Nearly choking, as she was just swallowing some tea. Rises.*) No, sir.

ROCHESTER. Nor mixed with intelligent people ?

JANE. (*With a slightly enigmatic smile.*) Never, sir. There have only been the pupils and teachers of Lowood and now the inmates at Thornfield.

ROCHESTER. (*Starts at the word " inmates." Looks at her quickly. Pause.*) Have you no fear of being overwhelmed by such continued gaiety and excitement ?

JANE. (*With a secret smile.*) I don't think I shall find Thornfield dull, sir. I am quite content.

ROCHESTER. Humph, you are evidently not exacting. See that you remain so.

MRS. FAIRFAX. Adele and I will try to make Miss Eyre happy—even though we cannot promise her much in the way of excitement.

ADELE. (*Quickly.*) Oh, but Madame, you forget, it is sometime very exciting here. Leah says there is a ghost in ze west wing—

(ROCHESTER *makes a gesture of angry surprise.*)

JANE. (*Smiles.*) Do you believe in ghosts, Adele ?

ADELE. (*Crossing to* JANE.) Leah says—

ROCHESTER. (*Angrily. Rises.*) Nonsense, if Leah says that again, she'll be discharged—(*He adds hastily to account for his anger.*) I won't have her frightening a child like you.

ADELE. Oh, but I have heard myself, many times—

ROCHESTER (*Furiously.*) Miss Eyre, take your charge to the school room. Isn't it time you began your duties? (*Crosses to* c. *table, puts down cup.* JANE *takes* ADELE *by the hand and they follow* MRS. FAIRFAX *out* L., *both curtseying. Their simultaneous curtsey will be funny. Calls.*) Go on, be off, both of you. Mrs. Fairfax too. Miss Eyre!—(JANE *returns to leave her cup on* C. *table.*) Miss Eyre—(*He severely indicates her belongings left behind.* JANE *gets her bonnet and cloak from chair* L.) I hope you will not allow this French monkey to fill your head with nonsense about ghosts. You don't look like a fool—but you're a woman.

JANE. (*Demurely.*) I don't believe I am more so than the average.

ROCHESTER. Well, the average will be quite foolish enough.

JANE. (*With an inscrutable face.*) Yes, sir. I agree. (*Curtsies. Exits* L.)

ROCHESTER. (*Crosses to door* R., *unlocks it and calls.*) Grace—Grace Poole. (GRACE *enters* R.) Lock that door. (*She locks it, then moves down* C. *He goes to below console* L.) Can't you do anything at all about that infernal noise? I thought you had managed to stop it.

GRACE. Have you ever tried to stop her doing anything she sets her mind to, sir?

ROCHESTER. I have a new governess in the house and I don't want her frightened away.

GRACE. Last night she tried to set the house afire and laughed when I caught her at it. Unless I punish her, I can't stop her making that noise.

ROCHESTER. "Laughed," did you say? It sounds more like revelry in Hell. The servants? What do you tell them?

(*Warn* CURTAIN.)

GRACE. That it's the owls hooting, but I can see that John the new groom doesna swallow it.

ROCHESTER. Well, those who don't can go! Mrs. Fairfax is the only one who knows the sounds come from a human being. By the way, what have you told her? Has she discussed it with you?

GRACE. No, sir, Mrs. Fairfax accepts what you've told her.

ROCHESTER. Yes, one is safe with a gentlewoman. (*Starts to chair* L. *of* C. *table.*) You're a good girl, Grace. Keep her quiet, for God's sake and keep your part of the west wing locked securely.

GRACE. Yes, and you keep yours. When you hear her, she has managed to outwit me and get into this part. I can't always be with her. I have to prepare her food and do other things. I can't keep her chained, though it might be better. She was mumblin' about you again. She'll do something terrible one of these nights.

ROCHESTER. You can't chain her; she is human, though God knows there's little sign of it left. Don't hurt her, treat her gently, but keep her quiet—and don't let her out of your sight.—And remember—none of the servants are to enter that wing.

GRACE. (*With a sly look at him.*) It fair wears me out—so it does.

ROCHESTER. I am raising your wages from to-morrow. (GRACE *curtsies.*) And Grace, none of the servants are to—

(*A frightful yelling and pounding at the* R. *door begins and increases through next speeches.*)

GRACE. (*Barely audible through the din.*)   My God, she has got down here again—I'll get her this way—

(*They open door* R. *and grapple with* MANIAC *as the* CURTAIN *falls quickly on* ROCHESTER'S *exit.*)

CURTAIN.

SCENE 2

Scene the same.

A morning in March. JANE *is leaning over the back of table* L., *looking with* ADELE *over her drawing lesson.* MRS. FAIRFAX *is seated on sofa with her knitting basket.*

JANE.   Oh, Adele, your circles look like oblongs.

ADELE.   Oh, Chere Mamzelle Eyre, I do not like to do ze circles. I prefer to do ze faces.   So !   (*Scrawls a face on her drawing paper.*)

JANE.   We must learn to walk before we try to run.   If you draw one perfect circle I shall keep my promise—you know what ?

ADELE.   Very well, Chere Mamzelle !   I will essayer—(*Becomes absorbed in her work.*)

JANE.   (*Crosses to downstage windows.   Stares out dreamily.*)   Spring will soon be here— The days will be like a glorious procession of passenger birds flying up from the South.   (*Sighs.*)   It doesn't seem possible when one looks at this snowy landscape——

MRS. FAIRFAX.   (*Over her shoulder.*)   You like the summer best, don't you, my dear ?   (*Smiling gently.*)

JANE.   Summer !   The hay will be got in, the fields round the corn-fields will be green and shorn, the roads white and baked—(*Crosses to fire.   Shivers.*) but it's not summer yet.

MRS. FAIRFAX.   Mr. Rochester and the Ingrams will have a cold ride this morning.

JANE.   (*Turns.   Crosses to* MRS. FAIRFAX; *kneels by her.   With pretended casualness.*)   Is he riding again to-day ?

MRS. FAIRFAX.   Yes, Miss Ingram and his Lordship are calling for him.   There is still no sign of his leaving Thornfield.   It is quite surprising.

JANE.   Surprising ?

MRS. FAIRFAX.   He has never remained here so long since I've been in his service.

JANE.   Really ?   (*Smiling to herself.*)

MRS. FAIRFAX.   He has been here six whole weeks.   I think I know why. (JANE *glances at her quickly.*) These increasing visits to Ingram Park——(*Meaningly.*) Mr. Rochester is a very great gentleman, my dear. We must both realize what a privilege it is to serve him. (*Pause.*) I am sure you feel the same as I do ? (*Eyes* JANE *with secret anxiety, not wanting her to be hurt.*)

JANE. (*Rises, crosses to below chair* R. *of* C. *table; sits on arm. In an expressionless voice.*) Of course.

MRS. FAIRFAX. (*Gently.*) I've noticed how kind he is to you. I am sure he never wants you to feel the slightest condescension on his part—but it *is* condescension just the same. Isn't it, my dear ?

(JANE *notices* ADELE *is examining her face in the hand-mirror rather than her drawings and is glad to change the subject.*)

JANE. Adele, it is not your face you should be admiring. That mirror is to help you in your drawing.

ADELE. But, chere Mamzelle. I like to look at my face. I find it very pleasing.

MRS. FAIRFAX. Listen to the child. It's easily seen she comes from Paris.

JANE. Give me the mirror. (*Leans over and takes the mirror.*) I shall remove you from temptation.

ADELE. (*Rises.*) Oh, Mamzelle, I am ennuyee of these lines and circles.—You promised to show me your drawings—— Plait-il, Mamzelle Eyre ! (*Coaxingly.*) Chere Mamzelle !

JANE. (*Rises; takes* ADELE *by hand and crosses to* C. *table.*) Very well, you have been a good girl, but afterwards you must really work. (*Puts mirror on table; picks up portfolio.*)

ADELE. Oui, oui, I promeese—— (BOTH *cross down* C. *to set line.* JANE *puts portfolio on ground.* ADELE *kneels* L. *of her. They are both facing the audience.*) Oh regardez ! Qu'est-ce-que-c'est, Mamzelle, 'ow it is beautiful.

JANE. That is a water-colour of clouds rolling over a swollen sea.

ADELE. Ooh, but it looks angry.

JANE. Yes, a big storm is brewing.

ADELE. (*Points to picture.*) What ees this—this great dark thing—there, look——

JANE. (*Taking* ADELE'S *hand away.*) That's supposed to be a bird. Do you see its wings ?

ADELE. Oh, oui, oui. And all that white there?

JANE. Spray and spindrift—Aren't they lovely words, Adele ? (ROCHESTER *in riding clothes has entered* L.C. *He pauses, and listens as* JANE *talks to* ADELE. ROCHESTER *crosses to back of* JANE *and* ADELE. *He gestures silence to* MRS. FAIRFAX.) All that drenching drags its wings down, so that it can't fly. That is like life, Adele. So many wings are trailing on the ground.

ROCHESTER. (*Suddenly, from the back.*) Were you happy when you painted those pictures ?

JANE. (*Quickly. Rises with* ADELE *and turns, facing him.*) Oh, I didn't see you there, sir.   Do you mind us having our drawing lesson in your library ?   Mrs. Fairfax thought it warmer than in the school room.

ADELE.   (*Crosses to* L. *of* ROCHESTER.)   And we 'ave also a more better light, cher Monsieur !   Look, how lovely !   (*Hands him the portfolio.*)

ROCHESTER.   No, I don't mind as long as I am not condemned to be instructed.   (*Crosses to* R. *of* C. *table; sits.*)

(ADELE *crosses to the rear of him.   Sits on the table.*)

JANE.   (*Quietly.   Crosses to table to gather up books.*)   That I can promise you, sir.

ROCHESTER.   Are you always so impolite, Miss Eyre ?

JANE.   (*Turns.*)   I beg your pardon ?

ROCHESTER.   I asked you if you were happy when you painted those pictures.

JANE.   (*Crosses a step* R.)   I was absorbed, sir.   Yes, I was happy, or as near as we ever come to it, I expect.

ROCHESTER.   You *expect?*   Then you hope little from this delightful business of existence ?

JANE.   I have *had* little—though perhaps all that there is.

ROCHESTER.   Humph, I dare say you existed in a kind of artist's dreamland while you were painting these—no doubt a master helped you with some of them ?

JANE.   (*Quickly.   But for a different reason from what he imagines.*)   Oh, no, sir.

ROCHESTER.   (*Ironically.*)   Ah, *that* pricks pride.

ADELE.   (*Crosses to* L. *of* ROCHESTER, *kneels.   Right arm around* ROCHESTER'S *neck.*)   Oh, regardez.

ROCHESTER.   (*Irritably.   Pushing her away.*)   No crowding, please.

ADELE.   (*Laying her head on* ROCHESTER'S *chest.   With both arms around his neck.*)   Oh, mais c'est mignon.

ROCHESTER.   (*Pushing her away.*)   Don't push your face into mine.

ADELE.   Plait-il, Monsieur—*Let* me see.

ROCHESTER.   (*Impatiently.*)   Take these off to the other table, Mrs. Fairfax, for Heaven's sake—(MRS. FAIRFAX *rises, crosses front to get portfolio.*) and examine them with Adele.   Leave these three here—(MRS. FAIRFAX *crosses to sofa.*   ADELE *follows.   Kneels by* MRS. FAIRFAX.)

ROCHESTER.   (*Examining sketches.*)   Yes—you have secured the shadow of your thought in this one; though probably only the shadow. You have not enough of the artist's skill and science to give it full being— (*Pauses.*)   I perceive that these pictures were done by one hand—was that hand yours ?

JANE.   (*Smiling to herself at his pompous manner.*)   Yes, sir.

ROCHESTER.   Who taught you to paint wind ?   There's a high gale in that sky and on that hilltop.

JANE.   I have watched the wind since I was a child.

ROCHESTER.   And where did you get your models ?

JANE.   Out of my head.

ROCHESTER.   That head I now see on your shoulders ?

JANE. Yes, sir.

ROCHESTER. (*Looking at her fixedly.*) Has it other furniture of the same kind within?

JANE. I think it may have and I hope better.

ROCHESTER. There, put the drawings away. (*Hands drawings to* JANE. *She crosses to table* L. *Puts them down.*) I am surprised they taught you anything half so valuable at an institution.

JANE. Oh, but they didn't. (*Pause.*) I was giving Adele a lesson— (ADELE *rises; starts to up back above table.*) hadn't I better continue?

ROCHESTER. It's Saturday morning. Let her have a holiday.

ADELE. (*Stops back of* ROCHESTER. *Runs down, throws arms around his neck.*) Oh, merci bien, cher Monsieur.

ROCHESTER. (*Irritably.*) Don't choke me! Mrs. Fairfax, remove this obstacle to my comfort. (*Rises.*) Divert her in some way, for pity's sake.

ADELE. (*Embraces* ROCHESTER, *goes* L. *to table. Picks up puzzle.*) Viens, Madame. show me ze puzzle you promised.

(JANE *picks up drawing tablet and starts to* L.C. *door*)

ROCHESTER. (*Goes below table* C. *Turns.*) So you taught yourself to draw and paint. Can you play?

JANE. A little.

(ADELE *stops on her way* R. *with puzzle and looks at* JANE.)

ROCHESTER. (*Sits* R. *of* C. *table.*) Very well, play—(*Pause.*) Please. (JANE *sits at spinet. With first a look of consternation at* MRS. FAIRFAX *who smiles and nods encouragingly.* MRS. FAIRFAX *and* ADELE *sit on sofa.* JANE *plays a few bars of Spring Song.*) Enough!—You were right, Miss Eyre, you play a little. Like any other English school girl—rather better than some.

(JANE *rises, obviously embarrassed.*)

MRS. FAIRFAX. Miss Eyre does so many things well, if she doesn't play expertly, it should not be held against her.

ROCHESTER. Madam, I am not asking for your opinion—nor am I asking Miss Eyre to play to me again. I shall manage very well without either. (JANE *to middle of* C. *table.*) You are displeased, Miss Eyre?

JANE. (*Wounded. Turns.*) I didn't expect you to admire my playing. I don't admire it myself.

ROCHESTER. (*Leans forward on table.*) You are too sensitive—or is it too vain?

JANE. (*Her voice trembling.*) I don't believe I am vain, sir.

ROCHESTER. I suppose you were accustomed to compliments from your director at Lowood?—Brocklehurst, wasn't that his reverend name?

JANE. Compliments? From that man?

ROCHESTER. Oh, come now, Miss Eyre, I've been supporting that institution for years.

JANE. It might be—wise to investigate where you dispense your charities, sir. No institution directed by a man like the Reverend John Brocklehurst is worthy of support.

ROCHESTER. But a Parson, Miss Eyre. I should have imagined that all you girls worshipped him.

JANE. Quite the contrary.

ROCHESTER. What? A novice not worship her priest? It sounds blasphemous.

JANE. I think he is one of the worst men in the world!

MRS. FAIRFAX. My dear, a clergyman!

JANE. I am describing him as an individual not as a calling, ma'am!
(ROCHESTER *laughs*.)

MRS. FAIRFAX. But, my dear, a man of God, you shouldn't really——

ROCHESTER. (*To* MRS. FAIRFAX.) This conversation, madam, is addressed to me. (*Rises, turns chair around, leans on back. To* JANE.) What did this Brocklehurst look like?

JANE. (*Slowly.*) Like a buttoned-up black tadpole.

ROCHESTER. (*Laughs.*) By God I can see him.

JANE. (*Moves a step to* ROCHESTER.) My first morning at school, he stood me on a high stool and told the other girls he'd been warned that I was a liar; that they were not to play with me. He told the teachers that my spirit must be broken.

ROCHESTER. (*Half to himself.*) They were unsuccessful. (*Looks at her reflectively.*)

JANE. I hated him so much I felt ill whenever he came into a room. When I was a child I could have killed him with these two hands. (*Holds up her hands.* ROCHESTER *looks at them and looks away.*) One morning he took it into his head to object to my hair. In front of the whole school, he caught hold of a mass of my curls and shouted at me that I must mortify myself in the lusts of the flesh. He spoke of it as an excrescence but all the time he kept hold of my hair, stroking it.

ROCHESTER. (*With a stern look on his face.*) I see.

JANE. Then he reached for a pair of scissors and cut it off. (*Pause.*) He made my girlhood a hell on earth.

ROCHESTER. I thought so. You *have* rather the look of a clipped young eagle.

JANE. (*Moves closer to* ROCHESTER.) I turned on him; I was quite little, you know, and pummelled him with my two fists, (*Beats him on the chest*) like that, right on his mean, bony chest.

ROCHESTER. You terrify me.

JANE. (*Suddenly realizing and ashamed of her emotions and the liberty she has taken. Turns and crosses to chair* L. *of table and sits.*) I beg your pardon. (*Sotto voice. Her head down.*)

ROCHESTER. (*Starts up around table.*) It evidently takes anger to bring you out.

JANE. I'm sorry. I forgot myself, sir.

ROCHESTER. (*Sits* R. *of table again and faces* JANE.) How did you happen to be in such a place?

JANE. After my father and mother died, I was left in the care of an aunt who hated me.

ROCHESTER. How old were you?

JANE. I was only five then, when I was ten she put me in a home for orphans.

ROCHESTER. But why a charity school?

JANE. My aunt lived in a great house, Gateshead Hall, but I was a discord there. I had nothing in harmony with Mrs. Reid or her dreadful children.

ROCHESTER. (*Musingly.*) A heterogeneous thing opposed to them in temperament. Not easily roused to laughter, not gay, not capable of serving their interests.—The recipe for complete and successful unpopularity.

JANE. All the same, I was glad my aunt sent me away. I didn't want to owe her anything more.

ROCHESTER. The bread of public charity was less painful.

JANE. (*Leans forward to* ROCHESTER.) The day my aunt took me to Lowood——

ROCHESTER. (*Interrupting. Abruptly.*) You've suffered enough; you must cultivate the talent of forgetting——

JANE. (*Eagerly.*) But you are mistaken, sir——

ROCHESTER. (*Coldly. Rises, starts* L.) You must not encourage yourself in these gloomy reflections.

JANE. (*Turns head to follow him. Rises. Puzzled.*) They no longer make me gloomy.—Really, I——

ROCHESTER. (*Another sudden change of mood. Rudely. A step to* L.) Well, their recital makes others so. I like bright faces around me.

JANE. (*Outraged by his injustice.*) Have you any complaint to make of mine? It is at least as habitually bright as your own.

ROCHESTER. If that is meant for repartee, it does not amuse me.

LEAH. (*Enters* L.C.) The riding party is at the gates, sir.

ROCHESTER. Tell them I will be with them in a moment. (*Exits down* L.)

ADELE. (*Rises; runs out* L.C.) I want to see ze beautiful horses.

JANE. (*To* MRS. FAIRFAX.) I thought you said that Mr. Rochester was not peculiar.

MRS. FAIRFAX. (*Smiling. Rises, crosses to* R. *of* C. *table.*) Well, is he?

JANE. (*Goes up* L. *of* C. *table.*) He is very changeable and abrupt.

MRS. FAIRFAX. (*Sits* R. *of table.*) He may appear to be, but I am so accustomed to his manner, I never think of it.

JANE. One never knows how to take him. (*Crosses up to mantel.*) He hurts one so. (*A half sob escapes her.*)

MRS. FAIRFAX. (*Observing her with concern.*) You will be wise not to let him affect you one way or another, my dear child. When he is married——

JANE. (*Shocked into turning suddenly towards* MRS. FAIRFAX.) What?

MRS. FAIRFAX. Why not? He is a man like other men, and not yet forty?

JANE. Of course. (*Crosses over* R. *below hassock.*) It's just that one doesn't associate him with domesticity—somehow.

MRS. FAIRFAX. My dear, you are so young and so little acquainted with men. I want to put you on your guard. I am sometimes uneasy at the way he makes a sort of pet of you—just a while ago for instance, the way he likes to draw you out——

JANE. (*Goes over to* L. *table to get drawing materials.*) And in the next minute snubs me as you saw just now. Do you call that making a pet of me ?

MRS. FAIRFAX. But did you see the look in his eyes when he did it ?

JANE. (*Turns.*) I didn't look at his eyes, his voice was enough.

MRS. FAIRFAX. Well, my dear, you are so discreet and modest. I'm sure you may be relied upon to protect yourself.

(BLANCHE INGRAM *enters* L.C., *in riding clothes.*)

BLANCHE. (*Imperiously. Crosses down* L. *of* C. *table.*) Where is Mr. Rochester ?

MRS. FAIRFAX. (*Rising.*) He's getting his things—he will be with you at once.

(ROCHESTER *enters* L.)

BLANCHE. So *here* you are, Rochester !

ROCHESTER. (*Gaily, after a swift look to see if* JANE *is listening. Crosses up to* BLANCHE.) You make the morning jealous—(*Kisses her hand.*)

BLANCHE. Papa and I have actually been kept waiting for two whole minutes. (*Coquettishly.*) It's a good thing it is you who dares to do it, Black Bothwell.

ROCHESTER. I deserve hanging for such a crime.

BLANCHE. (*Laughs.*) Then come at once. My horse is champing at the bit and Papa is becoming as hard to hold. (*With a sigh.*) But you know how difficult it is not to forgive you.

(*They exit* L.C., *ad libbing.*)

MRS. FAIRFAX. (*Sits* R. *of table* C.) Isn't she beautiful ? So high spirited, she just suits Mr. Rochester. He actually said to me a few days ago, " What if I had determined to put my old bachelor's neck into the sacred noose, Mrs. Fairfax ? "

(*Warn* CURTAIN.)

JANE. (*After a silence.*) Was he serious ?

MRS. FAIRFAX. You saw her just now, Lord Ingram's daughter, his equal in every way.

JANE. In mind, Mrs. Fairfax ?

MRS. FAIRFAX. Mind is not important between ladies and gentlemen, my dear.

JANE. (*Crosses to* L. *of* C. *table.*) Then what is ?

MRS. FAIRFAX. Birth—position—gentry must mate with gentry.

LEAH. (*Enters* L.) Mrs. Fairfax, ma'am, will you come and see cook. Butcher hasn't delivered and she's fair put about.

MRS. FAIRFAX. (*Rises.*) Dear, dear, that butcher. (*Crossing over to* L. *door.*) It's a good thing for him he has no opposition in our sleepy village. Yes, I'll come, Leah. (*Stops, turns to* Jane.) Excuse me, my dear. Why don't you go for your walk while Adele is practising? The rain has stopped. (*Exits with* Leah, l.)

Jane. (*Nods and smiles. Picks up mirror from* c. *table. Looks into it. Her voice low—and breaks toward the end of speech.*) Jane Eyre. (*Sits* r. *of table.*) You have nothing to do with the master of Thornfield except to receive your salary—and be grateful for his respect and kind treatment. (*Pauses.*) Be sure that's the only tie *he* acknowledges between you. So— (*Nods at her image in the mirror*) *don't* make him the object of your fine feelings, your raptures and so forth. (*Voice breaks here.*) Be too self-respecting—(*Low*)—to give your heart where it's not even thought of— let alone wanted. (*Strangles a sob.*) Yes, and listen, Jane Eyre, to your sentence! Go and draw your own likeness in chalk—and don't *compromise!* Draw it faithfully and write underneath—(*Weeping now*)— Portrait of a Governess—unconnected—poor—and plain. (*Sobs brokenly, head in her arms.*)

Curtain.

Scene 3

The same. A week later. Evening.

The r. *door is opened cautiously by* Grace Poole *who is secretly ushering out* Mason. *She listens carefully and then motions* Mason *to enter.* Mason *crosses to* c. *table.*

Grace. You can get out that way, sir, through the dining-room; one of the French windows is opened. You can go across the lawns and disappear into the shrubbery. There are wrought iron gates on the other side. No one is ever in that part at this hour. (*He gives her money and crosses to door* l. *She curtsies.*) Thankee, sir. (*In fear.*) Remember it's as much as my place is worth if the master ever finds out you came to visit *her*. He says you upset her.

Mason. Very well, very well. Don't tell him—he is a violent man. I only do my duty, God knows it's painful enough.

Grace. Yes, yes, I know. What do you think it's like for me? Day in, day out? Go quickly, or I shan't have time to lock this door— then there *will* be trouble. Quick, quick! It's Mr. Rochester——

(Rochester *is heard talking through* l.c. *door.* Mason *exits quickly through door* l. Grace *exits through* r. *door, but has not time to lock it again. This is important and must be definite.*)

Rochester. (*Off* l.c.) I shall want the horses at six—and breakfast no later than five in the morning. (Rochester *enters* l.c., *followed by* Mrs. Fairfax.) We want to reach London as early as possible.

Mrs. Fairfax. (*Up of* c. *table.*) Shall you be gone long this time, sir?

ROCHESTER. (*Crosses to mantel, picks up paper—opens it. Crosses to R. of* c. *table.*) Only ten days. I'm going up with Lord and Lady Ingram. They will probably rest here overnight on the way back.

MRS. FAIRFAX. (*Meaningly.*) And not Miss Blanche, sir?

ROCHESTER. Oh, yes, Miss Blanche is omnipresent. You had better prepare the Anne Boleyn suite for her. (*Smiles and* MRS. FAIRFAX *smiles also. Pause.*) Has Adele gone to bed?

MRS. FAIRFAX. She is waiting up to say good-bye to you and to thank you for her lovely ballet frock. She is in the morning room with Miss Eyre.

ROCHESTER. Oh! it's arrived? Tell Miss Eyre to bring her to me. (*Rolls hassock to beside chair—very carefully—as close to his own chair as possible. Sits—opens paper—pretends to read.*)

(MRS. FAIRFAX *has crossed up to door* L.C. *which she leaves open as she calls in the hall* "*Adele! Miss Eyre.*" ADELE *enters* L.C. *followed by* JANE *and* MRS. FAIRFAX.)

ADELE. (*Crosses to down* L. *of* C. *table.*) Oh, Monsieur—I thank you for my beautiful robe de ballet—et mes souliers et mes bas! Regardez— Look! Regardez! (*She pirouettes coquettishly, thrusting out her leg to show the stocking and shoe.*)

JANE. (*Goes to up* L. *of* C. *table.*) Good evening, sir.

ROCHESTER. (*Without looking up from his paper, but his hand shakes a little. Indicates hassock.*) Well, come forward—sit down.——

ADELE. (*Goes back to* MRS. FAIRFAX *above* R. *of spinet.*) Regardez.

MRS. FAIRFAX. Shhhh.

ROCHESTER. (JANE *moves hassock towards its former position.*) Don't move that stool, Miss Eyre. Sit down exactly where I placed it. (JANE *pushes hassock back. Sits.*) That is—if you please! Confound these civilities. I continually forget them.

ADELE. (*In ecstasy. Delighted at her frock—dances* C.) Oh, Ciel, Madame! Je crois que je vais danser. (ADELE *hums a song lightly and does a few simple ballet turns ending up on one knee in front of* ROCHESTER.) Mama used to do it so, n'est-ce pas?

ROCHESTER. Precisely. Now that's enough. Run off to bed. (ADELE *rises as does* JANE. ADELE *crosses to* JANE.) Mrs. Fairfax, cover young Mademoiselle de Montespan with a respectable nightgown.

ADELE. But I don't like ze respectable nightgown! (*Pause.*) Besides——(*Pouting and embracing* JANE)—ma chere Mamzelle Eyre put me to bed——

ROCHESTER. Do as you are told, Monkey——

(JANE *kisses* ADELE.)

MRS. FAIRFAX. (*Smiling.*) Come, Adele.

ADELE. (*Goes back of* ROCHESTER; *puts her arms around his neck.*) May I not embrace you, cher Monsieur?—You are going away to-morrow.

ROCHESTER. You may not. Be off—(*She dances out, blowing a kiss to* JANE, *followed by* MRS. FAIRFAX, *by door* L.C.) Coquetry runs in that child's blood, blends with her brains and seasons the marrow of her bones.

JANE. (*Sits on hassock.*)   You don't care much for Adele, do you, sir ?
ROCHESTER.   She's her mother's daughter.   That French mother who charmed my English gold out of my British breeches.   (JANE *stops knitting.*)   Yes, Adele is my illegitimate daughter—(JANE *starts again.*) Oh, I assure you she'll never know it.—I keep her and rear her on the Christian principle of expiating numerous sins by one good work. (*Pause.*)   Miss Eyre, draw your stool closer, you are still too far back. I can't see you without disturbing my position which I have no mind to do.   (JANE *pulls stool up to* R. *of his chair.*)   You examine me, Miss Eyre.— Do you find me handsome ?
JANE.   (*She is unconsciously studying him.*)   No, sir.
ROCHESTER.   (*Laughs.*)   By my word there is something singular about you——
JANE.   (*Embarrassed.*)   I was too plain, I beg your pardon.   I should have replied that tastes differ, that beauty is of little consequence or something of the sort.
ROCHESTER.   You should have said nothing of the kind.   Beauty of little consequences indeed !   Go on; what fault do you find with me pray ?   I suppose I have all my limbs and features like other men ?
JANE.   I beg your pardon, sir.   I intended no pointed repartee, it was only a blunder.
ROCHESTER.   Just so, and you shall be answerable for it.   Criticize me —does my forehead not please you ?   (*Leans back to show it.*)   Have I no bump of benevolence showing ?   Now, ma'am, look well.   Am I a fool ?
JANE.   (*Demurely.*)   Oh, no, (*Pause.*) you are a man.   (*Pause.*) Would you think me rude if I enquired, whether secretly you are a humanitarian ?
ROCHESTER.   Humanitarian ?   No, young lady, I'm not, though I once had a kind of rude tenderness of heart.   But fortune has knocked me about since and now I flatter myself I am hard and tough as a rubber ball—though there's a soft spot or two still.   Does that leave hope for me ?
JANE.   Hope of what, sir ?
ROCHESTER.   Of my heart's return.   (*Pause.*)   You look very puzzled, Miss Eyre, and though you are no more pretty than I am handsome yet a puzzled look becomes you.   (*Rises.* JANE *rises.   He takes the knitting away from her.* JANE *saves her knitting.   Her anxiety is funny.*) Young lady, I am disposed to be gregarious to-night.   I shall have little opportunity for quiet evenings presently.   (ROCHESTER *below* C. *table.*) Well, say something !
JANE.   What about, sir ?
ROCHESTER.   Whatever you like.   (*Pause.   Looks down at her.*)   You are silent ?—It's consistent.   I put my request in an insolent form.   I beg your pardon.   (*Crosses to his chair.*)   The fact is I don't want to treat you as an inferior.   I claim only such superiority as must result from twenty years' difference in our ages and (*Pause and a poignant change of tone*) a century's in experience.   I desire you to have the goodness to talk to me a little to divert my thoughts.   (*Leads* JANE *to sofa.*)

JANE. Very well, question me, I will do my best to answer. (*Sits c. of sofa having picked up her knitting.*)

ROCHESTER. Then, in the first place do you agree that I have a right to be a bit masterful, as I am older than you? (*Goes to up end of sofa.*)

JANE. (*Her eyes quietly on her knitting. Giving no sign of the turmoil within.*) Just as you please, sir.

ROCHESTER. That's no answer, or rather it's a very irritating and evasive one. Reply clearly.

JANE. (*Knits calmly.*) I don't think you have a right only because you are older. Your claim to superiority depends on the use you have made of your time and experience.

ROCHESTER. (*Goes to mantel; leans on it facing her.*) I can't agree with you as it won't suit my case. However, I admire your spirit and frankness. Few girls of your age would have answered me as—you have done. But I don't mean to flatter you; you may be no better than the rest. You may have intolerable defects to counterbalance your few good points—(JANE *smiles. Pause. Stares at her.*) I envy you your peace of mind, your clean conscience, your unpolluted memory. A memory like that must be an exquisite treasure.

JANE. (*Gently. Looking up at him.*) How was your memory when you were eighteen?

ROCHESTER. All right, *then*. No gush of bilge-water had turned it into a fœtid puddle. (*Turns head away from* JANE. *She fixes her eyes on him.*) I was your equal at eighteen, quite your equal. I was meant by nature to be a good man—and you see I am not. You would say that you don't see it—at least I flatter myself that I read as much in your eye! Beware, by the way, what you express with that organ. (*Turns up to mantel, leans on it with both hands.*) As for me, misfortune has caused me to degenerate. Dread remorse, Miss Eyre, when you are tempted to do wrong. Remorse is the poison of life.

JANE. Repentance is said to be its cure, sir.

ROCHESTER. (*Turns back to look at* JANE.) It isn't. Reformation may be—I *could* reform—But—since happiness is denied me, I have a right to pleasure—and (*With sudden passion.*) I will get it.

JANE. Then you will degenerate still more.

ROCHESTER. Possibly. (*Crosses a step to* L. *below mantel.*) Yet why, if I can get sweet fresh pleasure—(JANE *looks at him. He crosses to chair* R. *of table* C.) and I may get it, sweet and fresh as the wild honey the bee gathers on the moor—(*Looks back at* JANE.)

JANE. It will have a bitter taste.

ROCHESTER. (*Turns. Crosses a step* R. *to* JANE.) How do you know? You never tried it. How very solemn you look, yet you are as ignorant of the matter, as that cameo head. (*Points to cameo* JANE *is wearing.*) What right have you to preach to me, you haven't even passed the porch of life? (*Starts below sofa.*) Well, I have a dream now!—and even if it be from the devil—it wears the robes of an angel of light—(*Up back of*

JANE.) I think I must admit so fair a guest. (*Looks at* JANE *with unconcealed passion for the first time.*)

JANE. Distrust it, sir, it is not a true angel.

ROCHESTER. (*Tenderly.*) By what instinct do *you* pretend to know that? (*Goes to lower end of sofa.*)

JANE. (*Rises and turns to him.*) Your face warns me. Its expression is not a good one.

ROCHESTER. Good? Bad? I suppose your ideas on those two things are inflexible.

JANE. I hope so.

ROCHESTER. (*Goes to front of sofa to face her.*) It's all quite simple, eh? There are no degrees of right and wrong?

JANE. Degrees? How can there be? Either a thing is allowed by the moral law or it is not. And therefore one must not do it.

ROCHESTER. (*Bitterly.*) Wait until you are tempted. You will take the thing you want.

JANE. (*Shocked.*) If it is not mine to take?

ROCHESTER. (*Tragically.*) Yes, if the need is great enough.

JANE. (*Quietly.*) You do not know me.

ROCHESTER. We shall see—you are human, too.

JANE. To tell the truth, sir, (*To* L. *of table* C.) I don't understand you at all, I can't keep up the conversation.

ROCHESTER. (*To below table* C.) Where are you going? You're afraid of me?

JANE. (*Turns to him.*) Your language is enigmatical, sir, but though I am puzzled by it, I am certainly not afraid. I don't want to talk nonsense, as I might—being so utterly in the dark.

ROCHESTER. (*A tender note coming into his voice in spite of himself. Crosses to chair* R. *of table, puts left knee on it.*) If you did, it would be in such a quaint grave manner that I should probably mistake it for sense. Do you never laugh? I see at intervals the glance of a curious sort of bird through the close-set bars of a cage, a vivid restless resolute captive— if it were but free, it would soar cloud-high. (*She moves towards* L.C. *door.*) You are still bent on going?

JANE. It has struck ten, sir.

ROCHESTER. I am leaving to-morrow. Be kind and play to me— some simple air—I am in the mood for simplicity to-night. (JANE *goes to spinet. He lowers the lights.*) Music sounds differently in the half-light —my dear—come, prove your good will—(*To sofa; sits. Stares into fire.*)

JANE. I think it is more likely to prove *yours*, sir—considering your expressed opinion on my musical talent. (*Gives a soft little chuckle. She starts playing. After an interval, she asks mischievously.*) Are you suffering very much, sir?

ROCHESTER. (*In a queer, strangled voice.*) Yes——

JANE. (*Not understanding his meaning.*) But you brought it on your-self. (*Smiling.*)

ROCHESTER. No, this is one time that I—(MANIAC *enters through* R.

door, moves about in the half dark, sees ROCHESTER *whose head has fallen back, his eyes closed. She creeps up, going behind him, and is about to close her long claw-like hands around his throat.* JANE *looks up from spinet, sees* MANIAC. *Stops playing; petrified. Eyes still closed.*) Don't stop playing. (*As* MANIAC *actually starts to strangle* ROCHESTER, JANE *screams* "*no.*" ROCHESTER *jumps up in time to escape being strangled and struggles with* MANIAC.) Back, Jane, back for your life! Get Grace Poole—run through that door (JANE *runs out* R. *door and calls* GRACE POOLE.) quick, quick, she has the strength of a tigress.

(GRACE POOLE *enters from* R. *followed by* JANE; *she ties* MANIAC'*s hands behind her back and when she is quieted speaks but is getting the* MANIAC *towards door.*)

GRACE. You shouldn't of left that there door unlocked, sir. I've told you many a time. She finds her way all through our wing till she gets to this door. She even gets out the window when I lock her in the room. She'll do for ye one of these nights, sir, if you ain't careful. It's the one thing she's bent on. (*Turns to* JANE.) A deal of people, Miss, is for trusting in Providence. But Providence can't be expected to do *all* the work.

ROCHESTER. Take her away, take her away!

(GRACE *exits with* MANIAC, R. ROCHESTER *crosses to chair* L.. *of* C. *table. Sits.*)

JANE. (*Goes to* ROCHESTER.) Can't I do anything, sir? Who is she?

ROCHESTER. Every man has his private Gethesemane—his secret chamber. Mine is through that door!

(*Warn* CURTAIN.)

JANE. (*Kneels by* ROCHESTER.) Oh, forgive my question, it was not meant as curiosity. I'm glad you were not harmed. You should keep her better locked away. There are institutions——

ROCHESTER. I can't condemn her to that. They'd treat her cruelly and chain her. (*After a pause. Low.*) She is a member of my family.

JANE. I am so sorry. (*Rises.*) Good night, sir.

ROCHESTER. (*Turns—takes her hand.*) What, you are leaving me?— Like that! And you've just saved my life—at least—(*Holding out his hand, she gives him hers.*) I have pleasure in owing you so immense a debt, I can't say more. No one else in the world could have been welcome as a creditor for that obligation but you. I feel your benefits no burden. Jane.

JANE. There is no debt and no obligation for either of us.

ROCHESTER. I knew you would do me good at some time, I saw it in your eyes when I first met you—their expression did not strike delight to my inmost heart for nothing. My cherished preserver—Oh, Jane, Jane —so little, so helpless! (*With a cry. Struggles with himself. A definite pause here.*) Go, go away. (*He crosses to mantel. Suddenly.*) Good-night, Miss Eyre.

(JANE, *wounded, puzzled and mystified by this incredible dismissal, absolutely runs out* L.C.—*with a sob—as the* CURTAIN *falls.*)

CURTAIN.

ACT II

SCENE 1

An evening in April. Ten days later.
AT RISE: JANE *and* MRS. FAIRFAX. MRS. FAIRFAX *is standing near door of dining-room smiling and listening.* LEAH *enters* L. *with the silver coffee service.* ROCHESTER *is laughing with dinner party off* L. JANE *sitting on hassock at fire.* MRS. FAIRFAX *straightens lace cloth on* C. *table.*

MRS. FAIRFAX. It *is* nice to see Mr. Rochester so gay. Put it here— Leah. He seems to have enjoyed his holiday in London. Put it down *here,* Leah. Too bad that Lord and Lady Ingram and Miss Blanche are only spending one night. (LEAH *puts tray on table and exits* L.) They are anxious to get back to Ingram Park, I suppose. (*Fussing about with cups.*) Don't you admire Miss Ingram, my dear?

JANE. (*Rises. Ironically.*) I don't know which I admire more—her character, or her mind.

MRS. FAIRFAX. (*Innocently.*) Oh, it's her beauty, her style. Those are the things that will make her such a wonderful wife for a gentleman like Mr. Rochester.

JANE. (*Goes down front of sofa.*) Well, in spite of all these perfections, I'll be glad when such exalted folk have left us once more to the peace of Thornfield. (*To* R. *of table. Pause. Resentfully.*) I don't know why I have to be present to-night.

MRS. FAIRFAX. (*Lovingly.*) I told Mr. Rochester you were unused to company. I did all I could——

JANE. Then why does he insist on my being here when they come in from dinner?

MRS. FAIRFAX. I believe he likes you to hand the coffee, rather than John—He is always so clumsy.

JANE. That can't be the reason. There is still Leah.

MRS. FAIRFAX. (*Smiling.*) He may want you to accompany Miss Ingram on the spinet.

JANE. (*Decidedly.*) That I will *not* do. (*Pause here for laugh.*) Besides Mr. Rochester has already expressed himself in your hearing, as to my talent for *that* instrument.

MRS. FAIRFAX. Well, all I know is what he said—" Tell Miss Eyre it is my particular wish. If she objects, say I shall come and fetch her."

JANE. Well, I saved him the trouble.

MRS. FAIRFAX. Anyway, Mr. Rochester has not requested *my* presence. Don't be nervous, dear. Serve the coffee; they will probably not notice you, then you can sit over in the corner and they will forget you are there.

JANE. (*With an amused smile.*) Thank you, dear Mrs. Fairfax.

22

(MRS. FAIRFAX *exits* L.C., *closing door.* LORD *and* LADY INGRAM *enter down* L. JANE *backs to up of table* C., *and begins to pour coffee.*)

LADY INGRAM.   It's time we were leaving for Ingram Park, Percival. (*Goes to sofa, sits.*)

LORD INGRAM.   (*Crossing up to mantel.*) I am ready. Our bags are in the chaise—You and Blanche can just bundle in with your wraps.

LADY INGRAM.   (JANE *goes to* LADY INGRAM *with coffee which she takes.* JANE *curtsies.*) Yes, my maid is waiting with them in the outer hall. There will be no unnecessary delay once we have made our *adieux.*

(JANE *hands* LORD INGRAM *coffee.* JANE *curtsies.*)

LORD INGRAM.   (*Continuing, as though* JANE *were invisible.*) Deuced long drive up from London yesterday. Our host's beds are none too restful.

(JANE *crosses to downstage window.*)

LADY INGRAM.   They are less inviting than his dinners. Who is the young person who curtsied to us? She seems very efficient.

LORD INGRAM.   Only the governess for Rochester's ward.

LADY INGRAM.   Ward? What ward?

LORD INGRAM.   That French brat who jumped all over him, bawling for cadeaux when we arrived yesterday.

LADY INGRAM.   How fortunate he is. He has a perfect housekeeper too—Mrs. Fairfax, a distant poor relation.

LORD INGRAM.   Deuced convenient. He can combine charity, towards her with comfort for himself.

LADY INGRAM.   Such an uplifting combination!

LORD INGRAM.   Yes, one has the glow of good deeds and good dinners——

LADY INGRAM.   It will save darling Blanche such a lot of trouble. I think we shall hear the wedding bells before very long now, Percival. The child certainly knows how to manage her ogre.

LORD INGRAM.   (*Indicates* JANE.) Careful, my love, we are not quite alone. (*Takes* LADY INGRAM'S *cup, puts it on the table.*)

(BLANCHE *and* ROCHESTER *enter down* L. *He glances swiftly at* JANE.)

BLANCHE.   (*Crosses up to hassock and sits.*) And how do you like playing second fiddle to your daughter, my Lord Ingram?

(JANE *crosses to* C. *table, pours coffee.*)

LORD INGRAM.   I have long been accustomed to that position with your mother, my dear.

LADY INGRAM.   Tut, tut—you are master in your own house—or he thinks he is, Rochester. (*With a smile at* ROCHESTER.)

ROCHESTER.   Then why disturb illusions, ma'am?

(JANE *hands coffee to* BLANCHE.)

BLANCHE.   It's the very first time Papa has been known to leave the dining-room with the ladies.

ROCHESTER.   (*Gallantly, after a quick glance at* JANE, *to see if she is not missing any of his attentions to* BLANCHE. *To* L. *of* BLANCHE.) That was due to the impatience of his host—Miss Ingram.

(JANE *crosses to* ROCHESTER *with coffee. He waves it away. He does not even look at her.* JANE *to* L. *table puts cup down—sits chair down* L.)

BLANCHE. Flatterer! (*Taps him with her fan.*)

LORD INGRAM. When you are *my* age, Rochester, you will have learned to curb your impatience better. The port and walnuts will seem more important than the most beautiful of women.

BLANCHE. How charming of you, Papa! I declare your manners improve with your age. (*Smiling at* ROCHESTER.) Don't model *yours* on them.

ROCHESTER. My manners, as far as you are concerned, are in the keeping of my heart.

BLANCHE. By the way, Rochester, I thought you were not fond of children.

ROCHESTER. I'm not.

BLANCHE. Then where did you pick up that little French doll you have here with you?

ROCHESTER. I did not pick her up; she was left on my hands.

(JANE *does not even raise her eyes.*)

BLANCHE. But why do you have her living here? You could send her to a school and avoid the expense of a governess.

ROCHESTER. (*Coldly.*) I have not considered the subject.

LADY INGRAM. And governesses are such a nuisance. One can't fit them into any category. Besides they have all the faults of their class.

ROCHESTER. (*Icily.*) And what are they, madam?

BLANCHE. They are usually so plain—and so incompetent. But there—let's talk of something interesting. Don't you agree, Mr. Rochester?

ROCHESTER. (*Mockingly. With a killing look at* BLANCHE.) What could be more interesting than the subject nearest your own heart—yourself? (*She taps him with her fan.*)

LADY INGRAM. (*Rises; makes a step* L.) Dear Rochester, the day has been perfectly delightful, but we have a five-mile drive before us——

BLANCHE. Not yet, Mama. Mr. Rochester has promised to sing with me before we leave.

LORD INGRAM. Capital, my dear, capital!

BLANCHE. Come, Rochester, entertain me with your singing—I will accompany you. (*Holds out her hand.*)

ROCHESTER. (*Takes a hand.*) Who would not be the Rizzio to so divine a Mary?

LORD INGRAM. Yes, Blanche, let us hear how you make music *together.*

ROCHESTER. (*Hands* BLANCHE *up. Bows mockingly.*) Together, we shall lull even the nightingales to sleep.

LORD INGRAM. (*Yawning.*) I feel an affinity with the nightingales myself—(*Low to* LADY INGRAM.) 'Pon my soul, that's a good way to finish the evening.

LADY INGRAM. (*Low to* INGRAM.) I think I rather like the word *finish* in that connection. (*Yawning.*)

(BLANCHE *and* ROCHESTER *cross to spinet to sing.* JANE *starts at the sound of his voice; is thrilled; quickly looks down again.*)

LORD INGRAM. (*The instant before they finish. Clapping.*) Bravo! Bravo!

BLANCHE. (*Holds out her hand.* ROCHESTER *kisses it.*) Rochester, you deserve your reward. If you hadn't sung so well, I should have punished you. I have my methods, you know.

ROCHESTER. Alas! You have altogether too much power vested in you, my dear. A mere frown from you and I am worse than hung.

BLANCHE. (*Rises.*) Then you should not give me so much, Black Bothwell. But I will not hang you yet. I have other uses for you first.

LADY INGRAM. (*Crossing up* L.) And now, my own, we simply *must* take you home. I can't have our pet losing her beauty sleep.

LORD INGRAM. (*Eagerly. Crosses up to* LADY INGRAM *and exits* L.C.) You are quite right, Lady Ingram. We'll just pick up our wraps in the hall, Rochester.

ROCHESTER. My house will be a setting robbed of its jewel.

LADY INGRAM. (*As she exits* L.C.) Jewels must be acquired, my dear Rochester—when the setting is so worthy of them. (*Meaningly.*) They must be secured without too much delay——

LORD INGRAM. (*Off.*) Come, come, come, my dear, for Heaven's sake don't begin another conversation.

BLANCHE. (*To* ROCHESTER, *at the door.*) Don't you think Mama exaggerates my value? (*Archly.*) A little?

ROCHESTER. (*With* BLANCHE *up to* L.C.) I do not think it possible.

BLANCHE. You are becoming quite a Sir Galahad! (*Laughs, puts her arm through his.*) But don't idealize me—it would make life so dull.

ROCHESTER. (*Laughs sardonically.*) I will try not to. I promise! (*He glances towards* JANE *but her eyes are down, her face pale.*)

LADY INGRAM. (*Off.*) Come, Blanche!

(*They exit* L.C. *ad lib.* "Good-night." JANE *rises, picks up bag, runs front to get knitting from sofa—gets knitting and is making for the* L.C. *door when* ROCHESTER *returns and intercepts her.*)

ROCHESTER. (*Outwardly calm.*) How do you do? (*Crosses to* L. *of* C. *table.*)

JANE. (*Looking anywhere except at him.*) I am very well, sir.

ROCHESTER. Why did you not come and speak to me during the evening?

JANE. There was nothing I wished to say. (*Definite pause. Backs from table.*) Besides, you seemed engaged.

ROCHESTER. What have you been doing in my absence?

JANE. Nothing particular. Teaching Adele, as usual.

ROCHESTER. And getting a good deal paler than you were—as I saw at first sight. What is the matter?

JANE. (*To* R. *of hassock.*) Nothing at all.

ROCHESTER. (*Peremptorily.*) I don't wish you to leave yet.

JANE. (*Low.*) I am tired.

ROCHESTER. And a little depressed. What about? Tell me.

JANE. I am *not* depressed. (*Swallowing her tears.*)

ROCHESTER. (*Crossing up to* L. *of hassock.*) But I say you are—so much so that another word would bring tears to your eyes,—indeed they are there now, shining and swimming.

JANE. (*Crossing to* L., *below spinet.*) I wish you goodnight, sir.

ROCHESTER. You will do nothing of the kind. (*Pause.*) You find Thornfield a pleasant place? You can imagine it in summer?

JANE. (*Choking.*) It should be very beautiful.

ROCHESTER. You must have become attached to the house.—You have so much feeling for beauty, as well as a good deal of the organ of adhesiveness?

JANE. I am attached to it.

ROCHESTER. And would be sorry to leave it?

JANE. Very.

ROCHESTER. (*Crossing up to mantel.*) Pity! Life is always like that. No sooner have you become planted in a congenial soil than some rude gardener—(Fate, perhaps) uproots you, and you must move on.

JANE. (*Turns to him. In a voice of anguish.*) Must I move on? Must I leave Thornfield?

ROCHESTER. I believe you must, Jane. I am sorry, Jane,—(*Turns away.*) but I believe indeed you must.

JANE. Well, I shall be ready when the order to march comes.

ROCHESTER. (*Turns back.*) You do it very easily?

JANE. Would you have me distress you?

ROCHESTER. (*Crosses to up of table* C.) Perhaps I should not object.

JANE. I hope I shall never do that in this life.

ROCHESTER. The order to march has come now. I must give it to-night.

JANE. (*Ingenuous as a child is. Suddenly.*) Then you *are* going to be married?

ROCHESTER. Exactly; with your usual acuteness, you have hit the nail straight on the head.

JANE. Soon?

ROCHESTER. Very soon—and since it *is* my intention to take Miss Ingram to my bosom (she's an extensive armful, by the way) Adele must go to school and you, Miss Eyre, must find a new situation.

JANE. Very well—I will advertise immediately. (*Crosses up* R ; *turns.*) And meantime, I suppose—(*Crosses to* R. *of* C. *table.*) I was going to say,—(*Hesitates.*) I may stay here until I find another—home —to go to?

ROCHESTER. Certainly. (*Crossing to* L. *of* JANE.) In about a month I hope to be a bridegroom. And I shall myself, look out for a new place for you.

JANE. (*Low, almost in a whisper.*) Thank you.

ROCHESTER. (*Stands looking front by* L. *of* JANE.) Indeed I have already, through my future mother-in-law, heard of something that I think will suit you. It is to undertake the education of the five daughters of Mrs. Dionysius O'Gall of Bitternut Lodge, Connaught, Ireland. (*There is a sardonic note in his voice here and humour in his eyes.*)

JANE. That's a long way off, isn't it ?

ROCHESTER. Oh, a girl of your sense will not object to the voyage, nor the distance.

JANE. No—but the sea is a barrier——

ROCHESTER. (*Low.*) From what, Jane ?

JANE. From England—and from Thornfield and——

ROCHESTER. Well ? (*Eagerly.*)

JANE. (*Moves a step* R. *turns to* ROCHESTER.) From—(*Pause*)—the thought of Mrs. O'Gall and Bitternut Lodge strikes cold to my heart—it's such a long way off.

ROCHESTER. (*Whimsically.*) It is, to be sure—and when you get to Bitternut Lodge, Connaught, Ireland, I shall never see you again, Jane—that's morally certain.

JANE. (*Hiding her face. With a sudden cry.*) Oh !

ROCHESTER. I never go over to Ireland, not having much of a fancy for that country. (*Pause.*) I am sorry to send my little friend on such weary travels, but if I can't do better, how is it to be helped ? Come, Jane, (*Leads* JANE *to couch. Both sit.*) let's sit comfortably, this last evening we are together, like the good friends we have been. (*Pauses; takes her hand and looks at her intently.*) Are you anything akin to me, do you think, Jane ? Because I sometimes have a queer feeling with regard to you—especially when you are near me like this—it is as if I had a string somewhere under my heart knotted to a similar string situated in the corresponding quarter of your little frame.

JANE. (*Almost broken.*) Oh !

ROCHESTER. And if that boisterous channel and two hundred miles or so of land come broad between us, I'm afraid that cord of communion will be snapped. And I've a nervous notion I should take to bleeding inwardly—and as for *you*—you'd forget me ! (*Suddenly.*)

JANE. (*With a cry.*) That, I never should—Oh, I wish I had never been born—and never come to Thornfield—(*Weeping now.*)

ROCHESTER. (*Eagerly.*) Because you are sorry to leave it ?

JANE. Yes, I love Thornfield, I have *lived* since I entered it. I have not been trampled on, petrified—I have talked face to face with an equal for the first time in my life. I have known *you*—and it fills me with terror and anguish to feel I shall never see you again. (*Rises; turns* R.) I see the necessity of departure—and it's like looking at the necessity of death.

ROCHESTER. (*Rises.*) Where do you see the necessity ?

JANE. (*Amazed.*) Where ? Your wife——

ROCHESTER. (*Violently.*) My wife ? What wife ? I have no wife.

JANE. But you will have.

ROCHESTER. (*Passionately.*) Yes, I will, I will.

JANE. (*Crossing to* L. *below* ROCHESTER.) Then I must go. You have said it yourself.

ROCHESTER. No, you must stay. I have said *that* myself.

JANE. (*Turns to face him.*) I tell you I must go. Do you think I can stay to become nothing to you? Do you think I am—a machine without feelings? Do you think because I am poor, obscure, plain, little, that I am also soulless, heartless? I have as much soul as you—and more heart. (*Passionately. Backs a step.*) And if God had gifted me with beauty, I should have made it as hard for you to leave me as it is now for me to leave you. I am not talking to you through the medium of conventionality—it is my spirit that addresses your spirit, just as if both had passed through a grave and we stood at the feet of God— equal—as we are.

ROCHESTER. (*Seizes her in his arms.*) As we are!

JANE. Yes, and yet no. (*Turns; facing* R.) For you are going to marry a woman who is inferior to you and whom you do not love. I would scorn to do such a thing. (*Crosses* ROCHESTER *towards* C.; *is caught by him.*) Therefore I am better than you. Let me go.

ROCHESTER. Where, Beloved? To Ireland?

JANE. Yes, to Ireland. I have spoken my mind and can go anywhere now.

ROCHESTER. (*Takes her in his arms, close.*) Jane, be still; don't struggle so. Your will shall decide our destiny. I ask you to pass through life at my side—to be my second self, my best earthly companion.

JANE. (*Breaks, faces him.*) Are you rehearsing a comedy?

ROCHESTER. (*He turns quickly to listen, then opens his arms.*) Come to me, Jane.

JANE. I will never come to you—never.

ROCHESTER. But, Jane, I'm asking my wife——

JANE. I don't understand.

ROCHESTER. I had to be sure. (*Holds her to him.*) You have kept aloof, shown me only your mind, your beautiful bright mind—I've wanted your heart as well—you hid it. I made you jealous, I bored myself with these dinner parties, I forced you to be present—I flirted with Miss Ingram—right before your eyes——

JANE. (*Turns front. He holds her by her shoulders.*) It was unworthy of you.

ROCHESTER. (JANE *turns her head away to* R.) You strange unearthly thing—I love you like my own flesh. (*Kisses her.*) Do you doubt me now, Jane?

JANE. (*Happily—smiling through tears.*) Entirely.

(*Warn* CURTAIN.)

ROCHESTER. (*Back to her to look at her face.*) You have no faith in me?

JANE. (*Turns head away to* L.) None whatever.

ROCHESTER. Am I a liar in your eyes?

JANE. (*Mischievously.*) Yes.

ROCHESTER. Jane, sweetest soul in all the world—I entreat you to accept me as a husband. (*A far-off wail. Quickly turns* R. *to listen.*)

JANE. (*Turns to him.*) Let me look at your face——

ROCHESTER. Why ?

JANE. I want to read it.

ROCHESTER. (*Crossing up* C. *and returns*.) Jane, Jane, you torture me. Say yes, quickly—I must have you for my own, I must.

JANE. But why do you ask me to marry you, with such a crucified look ?

ROCHESTER. It's the torment of man in his cell of pain. For God's sake, accept me—come to me, come to me entirely. Make my happiness, I swear I will make yours. (*Holds her facing him*.) Jane, do you love me ?

(*Door slam*.)

JANE. With my whole heart. I think it a glorious thing to have the hope of living with you.

ROCHESTER. God forgive me. And let no one meddle with me—I have you and will keep you. (*Pause*.) Are you happy, Jane ?

JANE. For the first time since I am born. (*Weeps—as he clasps her, her head on his breast*.)

CURTAIN.

SCENE 2

SCENE: *The same. A morning in May*.

AT RISE : MRS. FAIRFAX *is arranging flowers at* C. *table*. LEAH *enters with vase*.

MRS. FAIRFAX. It's a good thing the wedding is to take place in the house; Miss Eyre won't spoil her little white shoes.

LEAH. Isn't it, ma'am. What a picture she looks in her bridal frock. I could hardly keep from telling her, when I fastened it on.

MRS. FAIRFAX. She seems to have grown quite pretty lately—happiness is a wonderful beautifier. Pity we can't have more of it.

LEAH. It comes from being in love, ma'am. Ah, 'tis grand medicine. (*Picks up rose—smells it*.)

MRS. FAIRFAX. (*Disapprovingly. Takes rose away*.) Leah !

LEAH. Oh, ma'am, I forgot to tell you, there was two men at door just now. Askin' if the weddin' was to be here.

MRS. FAIRFAX. You did not let them in, Leah ?

LEAH. No, I told them as how Master said no one was to be allowed in to-day, but minister. When they tried to argue I slammed door in their faces.

MRS. FAIRFAX. That wasn't very polite. (*Smiles*.) Some of the villagers have been gossiping; people are always so curious about weddings. I hope the minister won't be late.

LEAH. Never fear, ma'am. Mr. Wood ain't never been late for a weddin' yet—(*Crossing to table* L. *to put vase down.*)   Not even for ''is own, more's the pity.

MRS. FAIRFAX.   *Leah !*

LEAH.   (*To downstage window.*)   It'll be a sweet weddin' howsoever —won't it, ma'am ?   Look at sunshine !   Ooh, isn't it exciting ?   Goin' all the way to France, Miss Eyre told me when I asked 'er.   She don't say much, does she, leastways you've got to find out everything for yourself or else ask her flat.   But she's a lady all right, no two ways about that.   And, she'll be able to live like one now.   He has a great big fortune, 'asn't he, ma'am ?

MRS. FAIRFAX.   Leah, I thought I had trained you to better manners than this.   You must not discuss your master's private affairs.

LEAH.   You're quite right, ma'am.   But it all seems so romantic-like, it makes girl forget 'erself.

MRS. FAIRFAX.   That will do.   Go now and see if John is dressed in his livery and give a final brushup to yourself.   You are both to be present as witnesses.

ROCHESTER.   (*Enters down* L.)   Good morning, ma'am.   Isn't Miss Eyre ready yet ?   Tell her to hurry.

(LEAH *exits* L.C.)

MRS. FAIRFAX.   She is on her way.   You must try to be calm. (*Looks at him anxiously.*)

ROCHESTER.   (*Crossing to sofa.*)   Calm, calm ?   When my whole hope of life is at stake !   Go, go and send her to me—(ROCHESTER *goes back to spinet then down above table to sofa.   Shows signs of being at the breaking point.   Mrs.* FAIRFAX *exits* L.C. *after an anxious glance at his back.   After an interval* JANE *enters* L.C. *when* ROCHESTER *is by sofa.   He turns, gasps at the picture she makes, and opens his arms and* JANE *runs into them.   She wears a simple white dress and has a veil on her head.*)   Oh, Jane, Jane, that this day were over and you safely mine !   And no distance ever divide us again.

(*He embraces her—holds her off and stares at her.   She smiles up at him.*)

JANE.   But we are going to be married in a few minutes.   How can distance divide us after that ?

ROCHESTER.   (*Crosses with her below table* C.   *Presses her to his heart.*) I seem to have gathered up a stray lamb in my arms—that wandered out of the fold to seek her shepherd.

JANE.   We shall soon be on our way to France.   Think of it, I shall see the sea, the mountains—great cities.

(ADELE *enters.*)

ADELE.   (*Wistfully.*)   Are you going to take her away from me, Rochester ?

ROCHESTER.   Yes !   I am going to take her to the moon, I shall seek a cave in one of the white valleys among the volcano tops.

ADELE.   (*Laughing.*)   But she shall have nothing to eat.

ROCHESTER.   I will gather manna for her morning and night, the plains and hillsides in the moon are bleached with it.

ADELE.   She will want to warm herself—ze moon is cold.

ROCHESTER. Ah, but fire rises out of the Lunar mountains, my bird, and when she is cold, (*Picks her up and does a half turn.*) I'll carry her to a peak and lay her down on the edge of a crater—the crater of my heart. (*Turns to* JANE, *forgets* ADELE *as* MRS. FAIRFAX *enters quietly and leads her out as she chatters excitedly.*) Oh, Jane, Jane! You are like something out of the forest, an elf, (*Passionately*) a little thing with a veil of gossamer on its head that just hopped off a leaf—(*Touches her veil.*)

JANE. Whose only errand is to make you happy.

ROCHESTER. That is why I must go with this elf beyond the world, to a lonely place such as the moon, to the alabaster cave and the silver vale —where we might live—(*Low to himself*) in *peace !*

JANE. But we have no wings to fly.

ROCHESTER. (*Turns.*) Love is wings, my skylark! I will clasp a diamond chain around your neck, and a circlet on your forehead; for nature, at least, has stamped her patent of nobility on this brow. (*Kisses her brow reverently.*)

JANE. (*Freeing herself and facing him.*) Don't address me as if I were a beauty; I am your plain Quakerish governess.

ROCHESTER. You *are* a beauty; and a beauty just after the desire of my heart—delicate and aerial.

JANE. Puny and insignificant, you mean.

ROCHESTER. And I will make the world acknowledge you a beauty, I will attire my Jane in satins and laces.

JANE. (*Crosses to* C. *table—turns, faces* ROCHESTER.) And then you won't know me, sir; and I shall not be your Jane Eyre any longer, but an ape in a harlequin's jacket. I would as soon see you, Mr. Rochester, tricked out in stage trappings, as myself in a court lady's robe; and I don't call you handsome, though I love you so dearly; far too dearly to flatter you. Don't flatter me. Show me that talisman you have in your pocket—Put it on the fourth finger of my left hand.

ROCHESTER. With what a strange smile you said that! What a bright spot of colour you have on each cheek! Are you well, child ?

JANE. I believe I am.

ROCHESTER. Believe! What's the matter, tell me what you feel.

JANE. Do *you* feel *calm ?*

ROCHESTER. Calm ? *No !*

JANE. Happy ?

ROCHESTER. Happy ? Yes, to the heart's core. (*Pause—turns towards* L. *door anxiously.*) It's time that minister was here——

JANE. What is the matter ? Be at peace, my love. Nothing can take me away from you now.

ROCHESTER. You swear that ?

JANE. No, swearing is not being sure. I am sure.

MRS. FAIRFAX. (*Enters* L.) Excuse me, Mr. Rochester, the minister is here.

ROCHESTER. Ah ! Come, Jane.

(*They follow* MRS. FAIRFAX *off* L., *leaving the door half open. They are heard off—clatter of voices, ad lib. until* ROCHESTER *says " Well, I think we're ready." Ad lib. stops.)*

REV. WOOD. (*Off. Can now be heard distinctly beginning the ceremony.*)
Dearly Beloved, we are gathered together here in the sight of God——
(*As he begins, door* R. *opens and* GRACE *enters, sees that room is empty and motions to* MASON *and* BRIGGS, *the solicitor, to enter.* MASON *enters and crosses* L. *to above* C. *table.* BRIGGS *follows to* R. *of table, listens to see how far ceremony has proceeded, then returns to tip* GRACE *at door.* GRACE *exits. He watches her off, then goes* L. *to put his hat on spinet.*)

MASON. (*Very frightened, knowing* ROCHESTER'S *probable violence at what he is about to do.*)   Briggs ! (*Catches* BRIGGS' *arm.*)

BRIGGS. We haven't much time.

(MASON *puts his hat and coat on spinet seat.* BRIGGS *crosses down to* L. *door waiting for ceremony to near its question about " any just cause," etc. Note: This business takes place during the balance of the ceremony which has been continuing as follows:*)

REV. WOOD. (*Off.*)—and in the face of this congregation, to join together this man and this woman in holy matrimony, which is an honourable estate, instituted of God in the time of man's innocence, signifying unto us the mystical union that is betwixt Christ and his Church, which holy estate Christ adorned and beautified with his presence, and first miracle that he wrought in Cana of Galilee. Into which holy estate these two persons present, come now to be joined. Therefore if any man can show any just cause why they may not lawfully be joined together, let him now speak, or else hereafter hold his peace.

BRIGGS. (*Flings door wide open and faces those inside.*)   This marriage cannot go on. (*Exits through door, slamming it after himself.*)

(MASON *paces nervously up and down to door and as it opens hurries to corner up* L., *as* JANE *enters, veil in her hand, trailing on floor and goes and huddles on the sofa, her face stricken, staring in front. Door being now open, hubbub is heard—voices and indignant exclamations.*)

BRIGGS. (*Off. This can be heard as* JANE'S *entry has opened the door.*)
I tell you the ceremony is illegal.

REV. WOOD. (*Off. Low, shocked, incredulous voice—not at all the stage clergyman preaching in a superior manner.*)   This is a very grave charge, sir.

ROCHESTER. (*Off.*)   What the devil do you mean ? How is it illegal ? Who are you ?

MRS. FAIRFAX. (*Off.*)   Oh, how dare he ? How did he get in here, Leah ?

LEAH. (*Off.*)   I told you, ma'am. He is one of the men who came to the door and asked about the wedding.

ROCHESTER. (*Off.*)   By God, you'll prove your words. (*Enters with a quick rush towards* JANE. *Goes to* JANE, *stands* L. *of her.*)   Oh, my dear, my dear !

BRIGGS. (*Entering.*)   But I tell you I have documents to prove—
          (WOOD, MRS. FAIRFAX, LEAH *follow in.*)

REV. WOOD. (*Crossing up to back of* C. *table. Bewildered, shocked, speaks low as though overwhelmed by the incredible.*) Mr. Rochester! You have tried to do a terrible thing.

(Mrs. FAIRFAX *and* LEAH *stand in doorway trembling.*)

ROCHESTER. Wood, it is *you* who have done a terrible thing. You should have proceeded with the ceremony. What right has this fellow bursting in and interrupting a marriage?

(BRIGGS *to back of chair* L. *of* C. *table.*)

REV. WOOD. But I cannot perform a ceremony which I have just been told is illegal—without proper investigation. You know that as well as I, sir. You claim an impediment exists, what is its nature? (*To* BRIGGS.)

BRIGGS. Mr. Rochester has a wife living.

ROCHESTER. (*Violently.*) Who are you to thrust a wife on me?

BRIGGS. My name is Briggs, solicitor. My office is in London, in Arundel Street. I would merely remind you of your wife's existence, sir, which the Law recognizes even if you do not.

ROCHESTER. Then give me her name, parentage and home.

BRIGGS. (*Taking a paper from his pocket. Reads aloud.*) " I swear that on October 20, fifteen years ago, Edward Fairfax Rochester of Thornfield Hall in the County of Milcote was married to my sister, Bertha Antoinette Mason at Saint Luigi's Church, Spanish Town, Jamaica. The record of that marriage can be found in the register of that church. A copy of it is now in my possession. Signed, Richard Mason.''

ROCHESTER. If that is a genuine document, it may prove that I have been married, but not that my wife is living.

BRIGGS. She was living three months ago.

ROCHESTER. How do you know?

BRIGGS. I have a witness to the fact.

ROCHESTER. Produce him.

BRIGGS. Richard Mason——!

(MASON *comes down* L. *slowly.* ROCHESTER *makes a threatening gesture.*)

REV. WOOD. (*With an admonishing hand.*) Mr. Rochester——!

(BRIGGS *seats* MASON *in the chair* L. *of the table.*)

ROCHESTER. What have you to say? Come on, damn your soul!

REV. WOOD. Mr. Rochester!

BRIGGS. You seem to have overlooked the fact, sir, that your wife is not only the bearer of your name—but the sole inheritor of your property.

REV. WOOD. (*To* BRIGGS.) How does it happen that you arrive at this moment? Did you know of this intended marriage?

BRIGGS. We were informed of it.

REV. WOOD. But that paper, Mr. Briggs, have you the original marriage certificate?

BRIGGS. Certainly.

REV. WOOD. (*Shakes his head.*) This is all very shocking, (*Almost to himself.*) very shocking indeed.

BRIGGS. (*Takes out marriage certificate.*) I have the original certificate here, obtained by Mr. Mason.

Rev. Wood. I cannot believe—— Is this gentleman's wife still living ? Speak out please.

Mason. (*With a frightened glance at* Rochester—*hesitates, then answers.*) She is.

Briggs. Don't fear Mr. Mason—this is England and we have laws to protect your sister's rights.

Rev. Wood. Is she in this country ?

Mason. She is living in this very house.

Rev. Wood. Here ? (*To himself.*) Dreadful ! dreadful ! I cannot believe it.

Mason. I visited her here last November, without Mr. Rochester's knowledge. I am her brother.

Rev. Wood. I am an old resident of this neighbourhood, sir, and I have never heard of a Mrs. Rochester at Thornfield Hall. (*To himself.*) All this must be a bad dream !

Rochester. No, I took care of that. (*Grimly.*) Enough. Wood, close your book, take off your surplice. You can all go. There'll be no wedding. (*To* Mrs. Fairfax *and* Leah.) Away with you, outside ! —To the rightabout ! (Mrs. Fairfax *and* Leah *exit down* L.) Yes, I meant to be a bigamist, but Providence has checked me. I am little better than a devil at this moment, and as my pastor there will tell you no doubt deserve the sternest judgment of God. Gentlemen, my plan is broken up. It's true, I have been married and the woman still lives. You say you've never heard of a Mrs. Rochester, here, Wood, but I daresay you have many times heard the gossip about a mysterious lunatic kept here under guard. Some have decided that she is my bastard half-sister, and others that she's my cast-off mistress. Well, she is my wife, sister of that hero you see cowering there. She is mad, comes from an insane family—a fact, I of course discovered afterwards. She is also a drunkard. My life with her may be safely left to your imagination. Come, sirs, I will present you to the Chatelaine of Thornfield. (*To* Jane.) Wait here, I beg of you, if only for a little moment. Come, gentlemen. (*He goes to* R. *door—opens it. He exits followed by* Briggs *and* Wood.)

Jane. (*Rises, crosses to* C. *and speaks to* Mason.) Please go——
(Mason *tries to speak—she motions him to go.* Mason *exits* L.C. *Door slams off* R. *Screams are heard from the west wing, then silence.* Jane *sits* R. *of* C. *table after slam. After an interval* Rochester *enters* R. *followed by* Briggs *and* Wood. Briggs *below console up* L. Wood *above table* C.)

Rochester. (*Down* R.C.) That, gentlemen, was my wife ! You saw her spring at my throat. These are the endearments that solace my leisure hours. (*Pause.*) I wished to have this girl, who sits here so grave and quiet at the mouth of hell. Look at her ! Compare these clear eyes with those mad ones in there—This delicate body with that huge mass of corruption—This pure face with that vicious drunken mask—then judge me !—And remember you also will be judged one day. Off with you, both of you.

(BRIGGS *exits* L.C.)

REV. WOOD. (*In little murmuring waves.*) Miss Eyre—I am sorry—
I know you are without guilt—I—— If I could be of some help (.JANE
looks at him like a lost child.)—I am so upset, bewildered, I want so much
to—— (*He goes out* L.C., *shaking his head.*)

ROCHESTER. (*Goes to* JANE. Why don't you speak? You grieve
alone and you won't share it with me, I am prepared for a hot rain of
tears, but I want them shed on my breast. Come to me! I see no trace
of tears, only that white, crucified face! Your heart, then, is weeping
blood! Not one word of reproach? Strayed lamb that I gathered up
into my arms, God knows I never meant to hurt you! Oh, my heart,
will you ever forgive me? (*Crosses to below table* C.; *turns.*) No, you
shan't leave me, Jane. I read your thoughts. You won't say anything.
You're thinking how to act. I know you—I'm on my guard.

JANE. Could you think I'd want to act against you, my dearest?

ROCHESTER. (*Crossing to* R. *of* JANE.) No, but you are scheming to
destroy me—you're planning to leave me, to desert me—but you can't,
you can't. I'll have her lodged in another house, or we'll leave this
house to her. I'll give Grace Poole double her wages to stay with her
alone. (*Breaks and crosses below sofa.*) Now for the hitch in Jane's
character. Now for vexation and endless trouble. Jane, will you hear
reason? (*Crosses below* C. *table.*) Because if you won't, I'll try violence.
Child, child, you don't love me then. It was the rank of my wife you
valued. Now that I'm not to be your husband, you can't bear my touch.

JANE. That is unworthy of you. I love you more than ever. But I
will leave you.

ROCHESTER. But why, why? I shall keep only to you as long as we
live. We'll go to any place you like. Jane, you must be reasonable, or
you'll drive me mad.

JANE. Your wife is living. If I lived with you as you desire I should
be your mistress. To say otherwise is sophistry.

ROCHESTER. (*Crossing to* JANE.) I am not a gentle-tempered man.
I'm not long-enduring. (*Kneels at* R. *of her. She smooths his hair tenderly.*)
God, that you can be so sweet and so merciless! I know I should have
told you the truth in the beginning—but I feared your early patterns,
your instilled prejudices. I should have appealed to your magnanimity,
as I do now, and opened to you plainly my life of agony. My beloved!
I beg you on my knees by all you hold pitiful in the human soul—say to
me—" I will be yours."

JANE. (*Gently and sadly.*) I will not be yours.

ROCHESTER. Do you mean to go one way in the world and leave me
to go another?

JANE. (*Rises.* ROCHESTER *clings to her.*) I must.

ROCHESTER. (*Rises.*) Give one glance at my horrible life when you
are gone! What shall I do? Where shall I turn for hope? (JANE
turns away and weeps. He takes her in his arms.) There was never anything
at once so frail and so indomitable—A mere reed in my hands—I could

bend you with my finger and thumb, but what good would it do if I bent you and crushed you ? Ah—the wild, free thing looking out of those eyes, defying me. Whatever I do to the cage, I can never get at the bird inside. It is your spirit I want. You of yourself would come with soft flight and nestle against my heart if you wished—but seized against your will, you will vanish. Oh my heart !—don't leave me.

(Warn CURTAIN.)

JANE. I must !

ROCHESTER. You can't.

JANE. I will keep to the laws given by God and sanctioned by man.

ROCHESTER. No !

JANE. I will hold to the principles received by me when I was sane and not mad as I am now. Laws and principles are for moments like this one, when all my body and all my soul cry out to break them.

ROCHESTER. *(His arms holding her.)* My beloved !

JANE. If I can't believe in them now, it's because I'm insane.

ROCHESTER. Oh, Jane, Jane, don't leave me.

JANE. *(Holding him close. Kissing his eyes and lips hungrily.)* I must, oh my love, I must. Or we are both destroyed.

ROCHESTER. You condemn me to live wretched and die accursed.

JANE. We cannot commit this sin.

ROCHESTER. You think it better to drive a fellow creature to despair than to transgress a mere human law ?

JANE. *(Breaking from him. With a cry.)* God—God—please help me !

ROCHESTER. *(Calls in anguish as she runs to the* L. *door.)* Jane !

(She is sobbing passionately as she runs out the L.C. *door. It closes after her. ROCHESTER sees he is holding the wedding veil in his hands. Holds it up to his face a moment, then lets it drop to the floor. He sinks into a chair* R. *of table and drops his head on to his outstretched arms—his shoulders shake. There is no sound.)*

CURTAIN.

ACT III

SCENE 1

SCENE: *Living Room of the Moor House near Whitecross.*
There is a window in rear wall, R.C.; an alcove C with outside door at R; door
to kitchen C; door to upper part of the house L; a fireplace L. in the living-room.
There is a desk, chair and small table R; a chest beneath the window; a buffet R.
of kitchen door in alcove; an armchair with small table L. of it at C; a sofa
against rear wall up L.C.; a stool before the fireplace.
Dusk. Spring. A year later.

(*Wind low.*)

DIANA *is correcting school books at the desk.*
HANNAH *enters from kitchen with pan of peas to be shelled.*

HANNAH. (*Goes above table, turns.*) Gie ower studyin' now, do, Miss
Diana. You've been workin' ever since ye came in from school. With
a brother as kind as Mr. St. John, I dunnut unnerstand why he lets ye
work for your keep. Your mother never did.

DIANA. Mother did not have to support herself. Women never did
in her day.

HANNAH. No, men had " guts " in 'em once. They took care of
their womenfolk. (*Crossing L. to fire stool.*) It's time the little critter was
in. Walkin' on them moors, I suppose ?

DIANA. Yes, she hurried off after school to get her draught of air as
she calls it. But what a way to speak of Miss Jane ! (*Laughs.*)

HANNAH. Well, isn't she the littlest bit of a thing ?

DIANA. Yes, she's more like a porcelain elf than a woman.

HANNAH. She'd best get home before Mr. St. John be back from
London-town. He don't hold with her bein' out when that cruel east
wind be a blowin'. (*Slyly.*) He sets a deal of store by Miss Jane,
don't he ?

DIANA. (*Crosses to* HANNAH *at fire stool—kneels; helps with shelling peas.*)
She would be very good for my brother. She'd make him more human.

HANNAH. Humph, but how good be him for her ? (*Shakes her head.*)
The warm lovin' little critter she be ! Men be discouragin' to live with,
Miss Diana. I be wonderin' sometimes whether they're worth all the
trouble they gie us.

(*Wind up.*)

DIANA. (*Laughs.*) I dare say many women have. They pass from
their mothers to their wives, and they are only children all their lives.

HANNAH. Miss Diana, whatever makes them think theirselves the
Lords of Creation the way they do ?

DIANA. We've encouraged the idea—(*Laughs*)--for various reasons.

HANNAH. Your brother be late. The coach ought to be at Whitecross by now.

47

DIANA. I suppose it was delayed at some wayside inn. You know the driver likes to gossip with the ostlers sometimes.

HANNAH. Yes, drat 'em—and Mr. St. John's favourite Yorkshire puddin' duddled round the roast beef in the oven—I hope it don't go and overcook itself.

DIANA. (*Shivering. Goes over to windows.*) Listen to that wind!

HANNAH. Oh, my! For why does she go walkin' on them lonely moors all by herself?

DIANA. (*Closing her books—half to herself.*) It's where she takes her grieving and her dreams. She never speaks of it, but I sometimes think that hearts do break. (*Looks out at the violet-blue lights over the moors.*)

HANNAH. (*Busy with shelling peas. Rises. Between sofa and table.*) Oh, no, she never complains of nothing; she's always bright and kind and busy in the school and all.

DIANA. She doesn't vent her private griefs on people innocent of causing them.

HANNAH. You do put things so nice. It kind of dresses up everybody.

DIANA. One doesn't need to ornament Jane! I often wonder how I ever managed without her—or how any of us did, *for that matter*. When I think of that terrible night she came fluttering against our door in that howling wind, like a frozen bird with broken wings! And you nearly turned her away. That ought to be a lesson to you.

HANNAH. Aye, a cruel bad woman I was,—but she's forgiven me.

JANE. (*Calls from outside door.*) Who's at home?

DIANA. (*Turning towards sound.*) Because she understands people like you with her heart.

HANNAH. (*Opens door for JANE.*) Here she comes, all rosy and shiny, like as though the moor mist covered her in sparkles.

JANE. (*Enters front door; Wind blowing in with her.*) I've just come down from heaven. I've been flying with the furies and communing with the moor spirits.

DIANA. (*Laughs.*) They certainly have blown you about enough.

JANE. They gave me gifts—some for you, dear, and a sprig for you, Hannah. That is, if you don't scold me. (*JANE goes to fire.*) Ah! that fire. Life's contrasts certainly make its joys.

HANNAH. Indeed an' I will scold you. I warrant your little feet be all wet. I've got your dry slippers warm by the kitchen stove.

JANE. (*Sits on sofa. Holds up foot, showing sole.*) No. You can't blame a single thing on the moors. See. It's perfectly dry. I'm sorry, Hannah. Phew, phew, I smell something burning in your kitchen.

HANNAH. (*Running.*) Well, for sure case. (*Bolts into kitchen.*)

DIANA. We shall all find something to blame on *you*, Hannah, if you let supper be spoilt.

JANE. (*Gives flowers.*) Isn't this heather lovely? Austere and aloof looking—Just like the moors!

DIANA. (*Crosses up C. to cupboard; fixes flowers.*) Yes, cold and clean and sweet—like the wind up there.

(Wind down.)

JANE. *(Going to fire.)* It was beginning to be chilly though. The witches are brewing their potions of fate for to-night. The wind is rising.

DIANA. *(Crosses to window sill with a vase.)* Hannah worries about your walks on the moors.—She thinks they will make you sad !

JANE. *(Her eyes shining.)* The wind up there is wild music to my ears; it transports me into enchanted lands—far from reality.

DIANA. *(Anxiously.)* But aren't you happy with reality ?

JANE. Happy ? *(Wistfully.)* Isn't happiness just learning to do *without* happiness——?

DIANA. *(Crosses to fire to face JANE.)* It pains me to hear you say that. I had hoped that you were contented here—I have tried—to——

JANE. Oh, my sweet Diana ! *(Rises.)* I should be wicked if I were not grateful to my heart's core.—I *am* content with our home, our work, our peace. *(Seats DIANA on sofa, kneels to hug her.)*

DIANA. Well then ?

JANE. But for me—it is not enough to be peaceful—I need a purpose for living—I need a meaning—to—my life. Don't grudge me my rambles on the moors   I pour my yearnings out unto the wild wind and let its chanting turn it into song.

(Wind up.)

DIANA. You and St. John are both so restless. I wish you could be satisfied as I am. I love our little world here. Our work in the school all day—our quiet evenings at the fire, especially when St. John reads to us about those wonderful far off places——

JANE. Yes, places with magical names ! Samarkand !—Allahabad ! —Benares ! They thrill me, fill me with a wild desire to see them, to harness the wind that shrieks to me from the moors and fly away. *(Rises. Crosses to c.)* To lose myself in their witchery—and forget. Diana, do you hear that wind ? *(Turns below chair.)*

HANNAH. As for me—*(Runs in from kitchen.)* I hear the chaise that went to meet the coach at Whitecross. It'll be Mr. St. John. I'll run and help him with his bags. *(Flies out of front door.)*

(DIANA and JANE go to door.)

DIANA. *(Laughing to JANE as they BOTH run out door to welcome ST. JOHN. Off.)* She was railing at the nuisance men were before you came home— and now look at her !

JANE. *(Off.)* Was the coach late ? Let me help you with the bag.—

HANNAH. *(Off.)* Put bag down—I'll take it when I put t'other upstairs.

ST. JOHN. *(Off.)* Nonsense; leave them in my study. Oh, what a journey I've had.

(HANNAH enters to L. of alcove. JANE enters followed by ST. JOHN, then DIANA. They ALL re-enter the room.)

DIANA. *(Takes coat. JANE takes hat; puts it on HANNAH'S head.)* We were just beginning to be anxious. You seem to have been gone ages. One would think London were at the other end of the world.

(HANNAH fusses in and out with bags, etc.   Wind out.)

JANE. (*Laughing.*) Just look at Hannah. She is so excited that she's burned the Yorkshire pudding.

HANNAH. For shame. Now for why do you want to upset a gentleman that way? You know how they dislike their food spoilt.

DIANA. I suppose then that ladies *enjoy* burnt dinners?—or does not *that* matter? Oh, Hannah! You renegade!

ST. JOHN. (*Crosses above* C. *table.*) And now if you can keep quiet long enough, I will tell you all some good news.

DIANA. (*Moves with* JANE *to* R. *of sofa. Laughs.*) Ah! I *thought* he looked rather unclerically genial! (*To* ST. JOHN.) Now see how quickly you can tell it.

ST. JOHN. Let us all sit down and be calm and collected. (*He sits* C.)
(HANNAH *stands.*)

DIANA. (*Goes to back of chair* C. *With a comical look at* JANE.) Oh, dear! How reminiscent that sounds!

(JANE *crosses to down* L. *of* ST. JOHN; *sits on stool which she brings from the fire.*)

ST. JOHN. Don't hurry me.

JANE. (DIANA *kneels between* JANE *and* ST. JOHN. HANNAH *to* R. *of sofa.*) Don't you know more about the masculine mind than that?

ST. JOHN. Our uncle is dead.

DIANA. Is that the good news? He's never harmed me, poor man, and I haven't seen him since he went to America fifteen years ago. Are we really supposed to rejoice?

ST. JOHN. One doesn't rejoice at death. Our uncle has left us some money.

HANNAH. The Lord be praised!

ST. JOHN. The amount is not known yet. It is to be divided between you and me—and—a cousin——

DIANA. A cousin? What cousin have we?

ST. JOHN. One—Jane Eyre.

(*He looks steadily at* JANE, *smiling, and the truth flashes through* DIANA's *mind.*)

DIANA. You mean—Jane? (*Rises.*)

ST. JOHN. Yes.

DIANA. (*To* JANE.) But you don't look a bit surprised. Is it true?

JANE. It is certainly true that my name is Jane Eyre. (*To* ST. JOHN.) But how did you hear of it?

ST. JOHN. Didn't Diana tell you why I went to London?

JANE. Yes—she said your family solicitor wrote to ask you to come.

DIANA. That is all I *could* tell. (*Laughs.*) No one ever knows what bombshells solicitors have in store.

ST. JOHN. Well, this is a very pleasant one at any rate. (*Leans forward.*) He searched for this Jane Eyre; discovered that she had been deposited at Lowood Orphanage when she was a child—traced her as far as her first situation—then lost all track of her.

DIANA. (*To* JANE.) How strange that you came straight to us!

JANE. Oh, no!

HANNAH. And now we be all one family.

DIANA. Did you know we were cousins, Jane?

JANE. Yes—my aunt Reid told me as a child that my only other living relatives were a clergyman named Rivers and his sister who lived near Whitecross. I had always intended to find you. I wanted my own people.

DIANA. But why didn't you tell us?

JANE. I wanted to be forgotten and unknown for ever.

ST. JOHN. I am glad she did not. She gave us the opportunity of taking her to our hearts for herself.

JANE. Do you accept me as your cousin, Diana?

DIANA. With all my heart. Now we shall always stay together—all three of us.

HANNAH. Have ye forgotten how to count?—Three and one be four. I'm still alive and kickin'.

DIANA. (*To* HANNAH.) Let us go to the kitchen. This is even more important than Christmas, an ordinary supper won't do for this occasion. (*Kisses* JANE *and goes into the kitchen.*) A new cousin deserves something special.

(ST. JOHN *rises.*)

HANNAH. Aye—do you think I have nought stowed away? We'll cut the new ham I cured against Michaelmas.

JANE. And Johnny cake.

HANNAH. Aye and Johnny cake—and I've simmel cake and wine trifle. We'll eat like it was Sunday. (*Exits to kitchen.*)

ST. JOHN. (*To* JANE. *Goes to chair* C.; *leans on back.*) I have other news, which I did not give Diana. I want to break it gently to her.

Jane. Not bad news, I hope.

ST. JOHN. This inheritance means a parting.

JANE. But why?

ST. JOHN. I have longed for larger fields and wider labours than I can find in this parish.

JANE. (*Quickly.*) You are not leaving us?

ST. JOHN. Yes—in four weeks. I have taken my berth on an East Indiaman. It sails on the 20th of May.

JANE. But why are you so impatient to start?

ST. JOHN. (*Turns.*) When I was a boy, I paced these moors as you do now and dreamed my dreams in moorland loneliness—rebelled against the round of uneventful days—(*Goes to window.*) I have been like a soldier on sentry duty—(*Goes back to back of chair* C.)—wanting release—a chance in the battle line.

JANE. (*Eagerly.*) I understand. (*Rises, facing* ST. JOHN.) It will give meaning to your life. I almost envy you.

ST. JOHN. You do?

JANE. Your soul is something like mine, it craves adventure.

ST. JOHN. And service; I am going to India—as a missionary.

JANE. (*With longing in her voice. Crossing to fire.*) You are going to do a great work.

St. John. You could do the same——

Jane. (*Sits on sofa.*) No—I am weak, and not at all heroic.

St. John. (*Sits on sofa,* R. *of* Jane.) I could help you to cure the unhappiness in your heart.

Jane. Ah! If you could—(*Her eyes sad, as she looks out over the darkening moors.*)

(*The strange purple light from the moors shadows her rapt listening face as she turns it towards the open door.* Jane *is listening to the low, far-away wailing of the Wind. Strains of Sibelius music here blending with the low sad voice of the Wind.*)

St. John. Come with me. Help me to bear the flame of God into the dark places of the earth.

Jane. To India? (*She begins to listen to the Wind, her head turning toward the moors.*)

St. John. Yes—where your life can enrich others.

Jane. Oh, St. John!

St. John. I can engage another berth on the ship. We will be married before it sails.

Jane. Married? (*Pauses.*) But you don't love me, St. John?

St. John. You would be invaluable to me in my work.

(*Wind up.*)

Jane. (*Rises.*) Ah, you have answered me. (*Turns her face towards the sighing purpling moors thinking of* Rochester's *wild, glorious love. Turns to him.*) You see—I have *known* love.

St. John. (*Rises.*) You attach a false value to human affection, Jane.

Jane. (*Pauses.*) Perhaps I do. (*Pause.*) St. John, you *are* good, but with the terrible goodness of the unimaginative that would end by killing me if I married you—(*Pause. Crosses to window.*)

St. John. Come to India——(*Crosses a step after her.*) You can be of use there.

Jane. (*Half to herself as she gazes out.*) It's so far from England. (*A faint voice seems now to be heard from far off, through the Wind and the wild sad music.*)

St. John. Ah! (*Crosses to post by door.*) I know what is dragging at your heart, and chaining you to the symbol that is England. I learned your unhappy story from the solicitor yesterday. He told me everything about Thornfield Hall.

Jane. (*Quickly.*) Did he say if Mr. Rochester was well?

St. John. (*Stiffly.*) No, he only spoke of what that scoundrel had tried to do to you.

Jane. (*Sternly.*) Don't judge him!

St. John. (L. *of her.*) I don't want to judge any man. I only ask you to face your true situation. Do you hope for a change of circumstances that will reunite you to one who nearly ruined your life?

Jane. Don't— —

St. John. Has this love brought you any happiness? (*Wind and music swell.*)

Jane. (*Down* C. *a step.*) All I have ever known——

St. John. (*Stands back of her* l.) No. It was an illusion. Come with me and forget.

(Jane *to desk chair, sits.* St. John *to up desk; sits on it. The Wind is wailing and crying.* Jane *seem to be listening to it intently.*)

Jane. Ah—if you were right! If going with you would heal this everlasting pain——(*Her hand on her heart.*)

St. John. You can only find peace by forgetting yourself completely.

Jane. If I could be sure! (*Turns and looks at him longingly. Wind now very important. Music continues all through.*)

St. John. What is the alternative to my offer? An empty life—a little round of duties and a golden opportunity for a high adventure cast aside! I know you—I know I call to the depths in you when I voice the forces that drive me from within. I will take you to a new land, glowing with a strange beauty, over seas and mountains different from anything you've ever imgained.

Jane. Where I could drown my memories in work!

St. John. (*Rises, stands back of* Jane.) To have you by my side in my new life; together we could face whatever comes——

Jane. (*Questioningly.*) Whatever comes——(*Looking out to the moors. Music and Wind swell.*)

St. John. (*Calls.*) Diana, come and hear the happy news, bring the glasses in here. Jane is going to marry me.

Hannah. (*Running in with* Diana.) Oh, the dear children!

St. John. (*Exultant.*) Jane is going to marry me.

Diana. And the happiest news comes last! I've prayed for this to happen.

Hannah. (*Solemnly.*) She'll need a deal of cherishin', Mr. St. John —aye and not too much sermonisin'.

(*Warn* Curtain.)

Diana. We must pour the wine. Hold the glasses, Hannah!

St. John. No, let me.

Jane. Hush— Listen!

(*The room is getting dark, the moon is rising over the moors, an eeriness creeps into the room with the long, low, almost human wailing of the Wind. Music blends with it.*)

St. John. That is only the wind wailing on the moors. It always sounds weird and eerie.

(St. John *goes to kiss* Jane *on her forehead. She puts up her hand.*)

Jane. Wait! Did you hear it? (*A mournful wail like a human voice in the wind sounding like—J A N E—J A N E.*) Listen—don't you hear my name? (*Awed and moved to her depths. Rises and goes to open door.*)

Hannah. For the love of God, don't look like that!

St. John. What is it? What are you listening to?

(*Dusk now fills the room—the glow of the light over moors is eerie.*)

Jane. It's his voice!—calling to me in pain and woe—Listen!

(*Again the wild sad cry of the wind, and the voice.—Music almost unbearably sad—J A N E—J A N E.*)

St. John. Whose voice? What has happened to you? ·

Jane. (*Turns.*) No, I can't marry you, St. John. It *is* his voice!
Calling to me in pain and woe. It's a sign. (*Crosses to c. by alcove.
With a cry.*) How could I have forgotten? (*Her name is called again in
the Wind and music.*)

St. John. (*Sternly.*) Where are you going?

Jane. To him! To him! (*Catching up her shawl from chair. Runs
out into the dusk.*)

(*Music and Wind continue, and theatre kept dark for one minute after Curtain.*)

CURTAIN.

SCENE 2

The same as Act I. A few days later. Mrs. Fairfax *is seated on the sofa.
Her basket of knitting at her side.*

*The door formerly leading from this room to the west wing has been removed and a
large high window is in its place. (The west wing having been burned in the
interval in a great fire.) Through this is visible a lovely view of the orchards in
blossom.*

Leah. (*Calling offstage.*) Oh, ma'am, whoever do you think is here?

Mrs. Fairfax. Control yourself, Leah, who *can* it be?

Leah. (*Entering l.c. Crosses to spinet.*) Oh, ma'am—it's her own
little self all dressed in sprigged muslin—like a picture in a fairy tale.

Mrs. Fairfax. (*Rising.*) Who, who?

Leah. The master's bride that was to be, ma'am. Miss Eyre.
Whatever'll he say? Shall I ask her to come in?

Mrs. Fairfax. (*Turns and crosses and meets* Jane, *who enters at l. door.*)
Certainly! Jane, my dear girl? Why didn't you come before?

Jane. Tell me, is he well?

Mrs. Fairfax. He's in great trouble.

Jane. (*Starts to l.* Mrs. Fairfax *stops her.*) Yes, I know, that's
why I'm here.

Mrs. Fairfax. We searched high and low for you, dear. Your
going like that nearly killed him. But I understand; you did right, my
child, though my heart bled for you.

Jane. But what's happened to the house? I noticed as I drove up,
all the west wing is gone. Did he have it pulled down?

Leah. (*Crosses to l. of* Jane.) Don't you want some breakfast, Miss
Eyre?

Jane. No, no—thank you.

Mrs. Fairfax. (*To* Leah.) Don't mention Miss Eyre's arrival to
anyone, yet.

Leah. Oh, no, ma'am, not for the world. (*Exits l.*)

JANE. Now, tell me everything.

MRS. FAIRFAX. (*Crossing to lower end of sofa.*) We had a great calamity.

JANE. But, Mr. Rochester——?

MRS. FAIRFAX. (*Sits on sofa. JANE kneels facing her.*) Wait, my dear. Be patient with an old woman. A fire broke out in the dead of night six months after you had gone. The whole west wing was destroyed. That's why you see this window here.

JANE. But, Mr. Rochester——?

MRS. FAIRFAX. No.

JANE. Was " she " hurt ?

MRS. FAIRFAX. Yes, she was killed, and Grace Poole was suffocated by the smoke.

JANE. God rest their souls ! How did it happen ?

MRS. FAIRFAX. I'm afraid that Grace sometimes drank too much. The maniac soon realized this and used to watch her opportunity. The night of the fire she managed to get as far as your old room, which he had allowed no one to enter or touch—she set fire to your bed and then she went back and set fire to her own room. The house was soon in an uproar. Mr. Rochester got the servants out of their beds—their wing was ablaze. Then he went back to save his wife. They called out to him that she was up on the roof. There she was screaming and waving her arms and laughing madly, that long black hair streaming against the flames. He went up the skylight to the roof, I heard him call " Bertha "—We were all in the courtyard watching. We saw him approach her and then—She screamed and gave a spring—the next minute she lay crushed on the walk——

JANE. And he ?

MRS. FAIRFAX. Oh, my dear, prepare yourself.

JANE. Please, please——

MRS. FAIRFAX. The fire burnt his forehead and his eyes. (*Pause. Very low.*) He is blind.

JANE. (*Rises. After a pause.*) I am grateful that he lives.

MRS. FAIRFAX. (*Rises.*) Wait till he hears your voice, my dear. Never was woman loved as he loves you. He searched for you as though you were the most precious jewel in the world. After you left he became savage. He tried to send me away. I wouldn't budge !

(LEAH *enters with coffee from* L. *Puts coffee on* L. *table.*)

JANE. (*Kisses her.*) God will reward you ! But where is Adele ?

MRS. FAIRFAX. At school in France.

LEAH. He's comin' through the dinin' room, ma'am !

JANE. Let me meet him in my own way.

MRS. FAIRFAX. Come with me, Leah. Bless you, my dear. Be brave.

(LEAH *and* MRS. FAIRFAX *exit* L.C. *door.* ROCHESTER *enters* L. *Crosses to chair* R. *of* C. *table.* JANE *watches him groping to find his chair, her eyes wet with tears. He walks quickly, angry at his own stumbling—all his old fire still there—no stick to help him.*)

ROCHESTER. Are you here, Leah? My coffee. (JANE *crosses to him with coffee.*) It is you, Leah, isn't it? *Who is this? Speak!*

JANE. (*Tenderly.*) Shall I speak of how long it has seemed, and how sorely I have missed you?

ROCHESTER. *Who* is it? *What* is it? *Who* speaks?

JANE. I do. But you have not welcomed me yet.

ROCHESTER. But *where* are you? (*Puts coffee cup down.* JANE *goes R. of table.*) Or is it only a voice? Oh, God for my eyes! I can't see— But I *must* feel or my heart will stop beating and my brain burst. What ever or whoever you are let me *touch* you or I can't live. (*She places her hand in his.*) Her very fingers! Her small slight fingers! If so, there must be more of her! Is it *Jane?* This is her shape and size?

JANE. And her voice! She is all here, her heart too. God bless you, my love! I'm glad to be so near you again. (*Kneels by* ROCHESTER.)

ROCHESTER. (*With a great cry.*) Jane Eyre! Jane Eyre!

JANE. I have come back to you.

ROCHESTER. In truth? In the flesh? Or is it her spirit?

JANE. You hold me? And fast enough! Am I cold like a ghost?

ROCHESTER. *My dear!* This is *certainly you*, but I *can't* be so blest after such misery! I've had this dream so many nights when I've clasped you to my heart as I do now—and kissed this face, this adored face—and felt that you loved me—and *trusted* you not to leave me——

JANE. Which I never will from this day.

ROCHESTER. Yes, so the vision said, but I always awoke and found it empty mockery.—Gentle, soft dream nestling in my arms now, you will fly too. It *is* you, Jane? You have come back to me.

JANE. (*Dashes the tears away, kissing him tenderly on his blind eyelids— then sweeps his hair off his scarred brow, and kisses it.*) Forever.

ROCHESTER. But who found you? Who told you how dire was my need?

JANE. (*Low; knowing he will understand.*) The wind wailing on the moors——

ROCHESTER. (*In a strange voice.*) Then my call reached you?

JANE. Yes, four days ago.

ROCHESTER. Then there *is* a merciful God! Jane, four days ago at dusk I stood in the orchard and raised my face to the sky. I called on God to have mercy on me and if you were alive to send you to me. Then I called your name——

JANE. I heard it—and at a very critical moment—and I came to you. And if you won't let me stay with you, (*Laughs. Rises.*) I can build a house of my own close up to your door, and you may come and sit in my parlour when you want company of an evening. I'll be your companion and your eyes. Look happy now. You'll not be left desolate as long as I live.

ROCHESTER. But where have you been?

JANE. I'm an independent woman now.

ROCHESTER. No! I can't be heroic! I won't give you up. The world will call me selfish, but my very soul demands you.

JANE. You won't be consulted. I have said I am staying with you.

ROCHESTER.　Yes, but you understand one thing by that—I, another. (*Pause.*) I suppose I should now only entertain platonic feelings for you? Do you think so? Tell me.

JANE.　I will think what you like. (*Her head low.*)

ROCHESTER.　But you are young. You must marry some day.

JANE.　I don't care about being married.

ROCHESTER.　If I were what I once was I'd *make* you care—but—a sightless block!

JANE.　It's time someone undertook to rehumanize you. (*Sits in his lap.*) Your hair—reminds me of eagles' feathers. There always was something of an eagle about you anyway——

ROCHESTER.　I thought you'd be revolted at the sight of me.

JANE.　Don't tell me so lest I should say something disparaging of your judgment. (*With a deep sigh of content.*) Ah!

ROCHESTER.　A sigh, beloved?

JANE.　Of content. I'm at home again. With you I'm at perfect ease of all people in the world. You bring to life and light my whole nature. With *you* I live thoroughly.

ROCHESTER.　You're sure you're a human being, Jane?

JANE.　I conscientiously believe so!

ROCHESTER.　Am I hideous?

JANE.　You were never handsome, you know.

ROCHESTER.　Miss Eyre, you can leave me. Why do you remain pertinaciously perched on my knee—when I've given you notice to quit?

JANE.　Because I'm confortable here.

ROCHESTER.　But I'm no better than an old lightning-struck tree that lies out there in the orchard. And what right would that ruin have to bid a budding woodbine cover its decay with freshness?

JANE.　You are no ruin, no lightning-struck tree. You are green and vigorous.—Only just forty. Your eyesight is only a part of you—we may yet find a cure for that—Plants will grow up about your roots—yes, and lean towards you because your strength is so safe a prop.

ROCHESTER.　Oh, what a woman you are! Jane, you skylark! I want my wife.

JANE.　Do you?

ROCHESTER.　Is that news to you?

JANE.　I don't remember having heard you mention it before.

ROCHESTER.　Is it unwelcome news?

JANE.　That depends on your choice.

(*Warn* CURTAIN.)

ROCHESTER.　You make it—I'll abide by your decision.

JANE.　Choose her who loves you best.

ROCHESTER.　I'll at least choose her *I* love best—Jane Eyre—will you marry me?

JANE.　With pleasure.

ROCHESTER.　A blind man whom you have to lead about by the hand——?

Jane. With joy——
Rochester. Truly, Jane?
Jane. Most truly.
Rochester. Oh, my heart! God bless and reward you.
Jane. If I ever did a good deed in my life, I am rewarded now. To be your wife is for me to be as happy as I can be on earth.
Rochester. (*Humbly.*) Because you delight in sacrifice?
Jane. (*Rises and faces him.*) What do I sacrifice? Famine for food. To be privileged to put my arms around what I value—to press my lips to those I love—to repose on what I trust? Is that to make a sacrifice? If so, then certainly I delight in it.
Rochester. But my infirmities, Jane; and all my faults?
Jane. There *are* none, to me. I love you better now, when I can really be useful to you, than I did in your state of proud independence when you disdained every role but that of the giver and protector.
Rochester. (*Rises. Holds* Jane *in his arms.*) I have hated to be helped—to be led—But your soft ministries will be a perpetual joy. Jane suits me; do I suit her? (*Masterfully. Now that he is sure she is not marrying him out of pity he stands upright—holds her off.*)
Jane. To the finest fibre of my nature.
Rochester. Kiss me, heart of my heart!
Jane. (*Tremulously.*) Oh, thank you, Mr. Rochester. (*Rising on her tiptoes—her arms round his neck. She gives him her lips. He clasps her to his heart.*)

CURTAIN.

PROPERTY PLOT

ACT I

Scene 1

Curtains drawn at window. Fire burning brightly in fireplace.
Electric taper for Leah.
Key each for Rochester and Grace Poole.
Spinet and stool to R.

Scene 2

Add drawing materials to table R.
Portfolio and water colour drawings against leg of chair, L. of table.
Tobacco jar and churchwarden pipe on table L. of armchair for Rochester.
Hand mirror on table with drawing materials.
Child's puzzle for Adele.
Open curtains at windows.

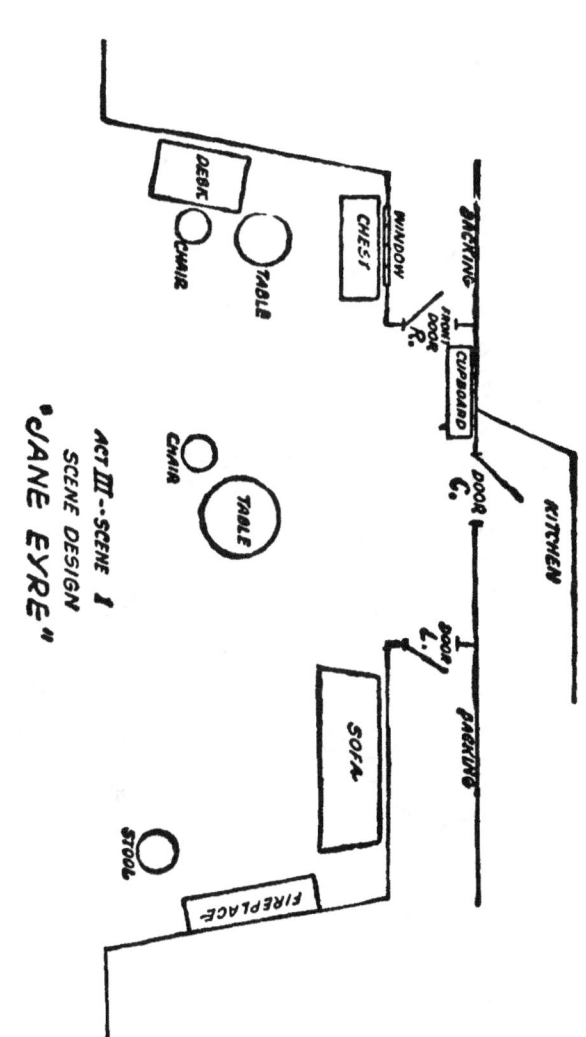

ACT III -- SCENE 1
SCENE DESIGN
"JANE EYRE"

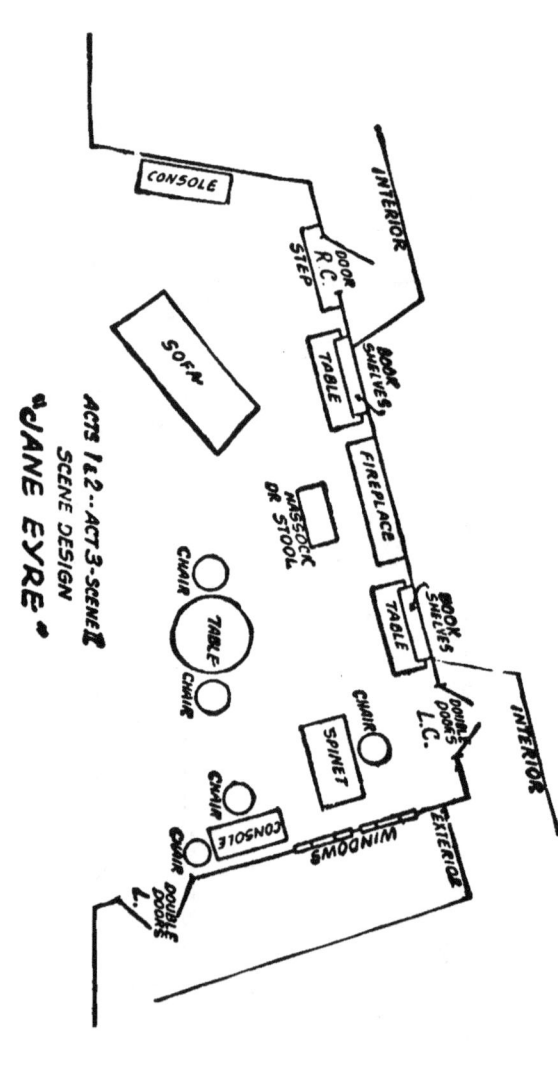

ACTS 1 & 2 -- ACT 3 -- SCENE II
SCENE DESIGN
"JANE EYRE"

SCENE 9

Strike painting materials, pipe and tobacco jar.
Add footstool for ROCHESTER to move and JANE to sit on.
Add London *Times* for ROCHESTER to pretend to read.
Close curtains.

ACT II

SCENE 1

Add big silver coffee service (Off Stage, for LEAH to carry on).
Add knitting for JANE.

SCENE 2

Add lots of flowers, some for decorating walls, other for vases.
Gay colours, and a bowl of roses to upstage end of table up R.
Ring in case for ROCHESTER's pocket.
Documents, wedding certificate for WOOD and BRIGGS.
Key for ROCHESTER.

ACT III

SCENE 1

Pan of peas for HANNAH to shell.
Flowers for table.
Sprays of heather for JANE (off stage).
Bag for ST. JOHN (off stage).
Shawl for JANE's head (off stage).
Curtains open and moors visible with changing lights as scene progresses deepening to rose, violet blue, and then dusk.
Wind machine (off stage) and ROCHESTER's voice mingling with it at the end.

SCENE 2

Back to Thornfield Hall.
A mullioned window up R. in place of west wing door. This is wide open giving view of orchard in bloom.
Table up R. from behind sofa and add vase of blossom.
Table from L. of armchair to upstage R. corner of it.
(Off stage, Tray with pot of coffee. One cup for LEAH to bring on.)

PUBLICITY THROUGH YOUR LOCAL PAPERS

THE press can be an immense help in giving publicity to your productions. In this belief we submit a number of suggested press notes which may be used either as they stand or changed to suit your own ideas and submitted to the local press.

CHARLOTTE BRONTË

Rushed into print and apparently immortality, the original manuscript of *Jane Eyre* was immediately recognized by the publishers who read it ninety years ago as a piece of merchandize that would move fast and bring in a profit.

"Daring," "virile," "highly sensational," and even "shocking" were the Victorian sales adjectives they applied to it. The public reacted by clamouring for a second edition within a few weeks, in the face of the more conservative book-reviewers' damnation of the novel as "irreligious."

To its author's career this success was as crucial as a lifebelt to a floundering swimmer. Six publishers rejected an earlier novel and only two copies of a previously published book of verse had ever been sold.

British press and public were certain this new novelist was a man. The reviewer of the *Quarterly* asserted: "If we ascribe the book to a woman at all, we have no alternative but to ascribe it to one who has, for some sufficient reason, long forfeited the society of her own sex."

In answer, the author wrote a fighting preface to the second edition, pointing out that "conventionality is not morality. Self-righteousness is not religion. To attack the first is not to assail the last——"

The publishers were delighted to print this lusty retort and not until a scandal threatened did they discover that Mr. Currer Bell, their best-seller author was a shy little "spinster" woman, thirty years of age, who lived in the Haworth Parsonage in Yorkshire, and was known by the name of Charlotte Brontë.

Their astonishment was in ratio to that of the gasping and incredulous public which was stunned to discover that an unmarried woman, or indeed, any decent, delicate, reticent female at all, could be guilty of the revelations to be found in that fast-selling, "improper" novel, *Jane Eyre*.

To-day the public is still amazed, not by the impassioned auto-biographical story but by the superb achievement of this woman who wrought her masterpiece in the face of poverty, isolation and the alarming ill-health of her immediate family.

One of six motherless children who made a grim struggle for existence at the edge of the most desolate of moors, Charlotte Brontë and her brothers and sisters were left to their own devices for toys, games or any sort of amusement. Of Irish stock through their curate father, Patrick

Brontë, and of Cornish lineage through their mother they were fortunately endowed with imaginations which developed markedly in the three sisters, Emily, Ann and Charlotte, and which proved inexhaustible substitutes for the toys they lacked.

The parsonage where they lived out on the edge of the empty moors had uncarpeted stone floors sprinkled with sand. Both food and clothes were scarce. While still no more than tots fit for kindergarten and council school, the four eldest girls were sent off to board at an institution which Charlotte Brontë later denounced to the world as horridly scandalous. Here two of the girls died from improper care and lack of nourishment. In spite of this tragedy, the detached and unmindful curate continued to keep Charlotte and Ann in the school until they, too, became ill. Finally, at the truly alarming state of their health, he reluctantly brought them home.

Back on the moors for five years, Charlotte, her two sisters and brother, Bramwell, remained busy with housework during the day, and with writing and story telling at night.

" JANE EYRE " AS A NOVEL

Labelled at the time of its publication a novel of " revolt," Charlotte Brontë's *Jane Eyre* is still regarded as one of the first feministic documents of the last century because in it, for the first time, a woman had the temerity to lay bare her heart and soul in the public prints.

In the transposition of this great novel to the stage no liberties have been taken with story or characterizations.

Had the character of Jane Eyre not come alive on the printed page it might have been an unthinkable task to lift anything but a stilted, old-fashioned, effigy from book to stage. But because Charlotte Brontë's heroine is essentially real and human, and of the stuff of which immortality is made, did this highly individualized young lady of 1847 fairly leap from its dog-eared covers to the English stage of 1936 and, the American stage of 1937.

" JANE EYRE " AS A PLAY

With characters as alive as these it is little wonder that the novel cried out for dramatization almost a century before Helen Jerome fashioned her present play from the Brontë novel. Three years after Charlotte Brontë's book was published a crudely written play was made from it which, nevertheless, was charged with some of the power of the Brontë narrative—proven by its subsequent thirty years on the American stage.

The first performance of this early dramatization of *Jane Eyre* took place at the Bowery Theatre in New York on the evening of March 26th, 1850. The parts of Jane Eyre and Mr. Rochester were played by Miss C. C. Wemyss and John Gilbert, two prominent actors of the time.

Abroad, it flourished simultaneously. The German version was brought to New York and first performed in October, 1854, by a

German company at the Stadt Theatre in New York and called *Die Waise von Lowood*, or *The Orphan of Lowood*, the notorious school where Jane suffered in the early chapters of the book.

Laura Keene, remembered by history for her performance in *Our American Cousin* on the night President Lincoln was fatally shot, produced the play on May 26th, 1856, at the Metropolitan, which she had rechristened " Laura Keene's Varieties." Her dramatic version of the novel was called *Jane Eyre; or The Orphan of Lowood*, and was written by John Brougham, a dashing actor and prolific playwright accredited with supplying Dion Boucicault with the plot of *London Assurance*. He had brought the script with him from England. Twenty-one years later the unforgettable Clara Morris included *Jane Eyre* as a standard role in her repertory and scored a triumphant success in it at Wallack's Theatre in 1877.

Marie Seebach, vaunted in 1871 as the finest European actress visiting America after Rachel, played *Jane Eyre* in German at the 14th Street Theatre where Eva LeGallienne later instituted her Civic Repertory.

Skipping along another fourteen years, this hardy perennial was still stirring audiences all over the country, this time with Charlotte Thompson in the piece. Maggie Mitchell, her widely disputed rival, scored in *Jane Eyre* until the end of the eighties and it was a moot question whether her adoring audiences were more devoted to her characterization of the heroine than that of Charlotte Thompson's.

Even the screen has presented a version of *Jane Eyre*. With such a persistently lively record to chart up, it is little wonder that Helen Jerome found this fertile melodrama convincing theatre material to-day.

HELEN JEROME

In an orchestra seat in the Guild Theatre some years ago sat Helen Jerome watching the play, as detached from its operation as any other member of the audience. To-day when Helen Jerome goes to the theatre she is critical of trifles and alert to nuances that never before touched her. Having once plunged a finger in the pie of play-making, her theatre reactions underwent a complete renovation.

It was the production of her first play that drew the line of demarcation,—that dramatization of Jane Austen's *Pride and Prejudice* which won acclaim in New York, London and in American cities " on the road." Actually *Charlotte Corday* was the first play she wrote although not the first to be produced. Next came *Limelight* which was presented at the Birmingham Repertory Theatre. *Jane Eyre*, her dramatization of the Charlotte Brontë novel was also first produced in Birmingham, and by Sir Barry Jackson. Next, it was done in the Malvern Festival in the summer of 1936. Thirdly, it found its way to London where it ran for a year at the Queen's Theatre. Later, under the banner of The Theatre Guild it came to America.

Helen Jerome is English by birth. She has lived in America for the last ten years, and is now an American.

www.ingramcontent.com/pod-product-compliance
Lightning Source LLC
Chambersburg PA
CBHW052239200626
46817CB00026B/3033